Anything for You, Ma'am

Praise for *Anything for You, Ma'am*

'Tushar has this instinctive ability to hold your attention with narrative deviations that illuminate disparate subjects...the charm of campus life, pig-headed professors, the advantage of sisters, the adventure of train travel in India, the joy of an early winter in Delhi...What Raheja does is to very cleverly localise the Wooster persona. So English aristocracy, the idle rich, the lad sent down from Oxford, the young man with great expectations and little ability, the chappie whose only survival tool is a smart gentleman's gentleman called Jeeves – all this is turned into rich material for humour of a local kind...Some of the humour is side splitting...'

The Hindu

'Remember Bertie Wooster?...the humour – most often arising out of situations poor Bertie gets himself into... *Anything For You, Ma'am* works on the same lines...Well, it would be too presumptuous to compare a fourth year IIT student Tushar Raheja's attempt at witty writing to a classic Wodehouse, but he does manage to get some laughs...a laugh-a-minute book...'

The Times of India

'Raheja writes a touching book about a young lover's story...that engrosses the reader, with its high speed rather hilarious turn of events... Amidst all the chaos are the sweet love moments...be it their date or their telephonic conversation...It is the story of a boy-next-door, which any youngster can relate to. Raheja moves back and forth in time, reminding one of ace writers like Virginia Woolf and Amitav Ghosh…'

The Pioneer

'The difference lies in the treatment of the subject…the narrative is devoid of lofty idealism…the lingo and its texture is very close to what students use in colleges…a good attempt by someone writing only his first novel…'

Hindustan Times

'*Anything For You, Ma'am* is a delicacy of feelings with dollops of mischief and fun…Infused with the sepia-tinted fragrance of life at IIT Delhi campus and turbulent love terrain of tweeny days, the book is for those who are romantics-at-heart and nostalgic about the good ol' college days…'

Society Magazine

'With all the masala of a Hindi movie, the story has interesting plots, interspersed with humour, enough to keep you glued to the pages…'

New Indian Express

'The author smears Tejas' life philosophy with a veneer of middle-class respectability and manages to bolster the book with the help of an extremely indulgent plot…one must hand it to the young author for an enterprising race to the finish…'

Deccan Herald

'The story takes many intriguing turns. It has been penned in a language that is perfectly suitable for a story placed against a campus background, perfectly setting the mood and verisimilitude… an enjoyable read…

Seventeen

'As one goes through the book, there is just one feeling that a reader gets. The feeling that a movie is being screened before him, scene by scene…'

Vijay Times

Anything for You, Ma'am

Tushar Raheja

RUPA
PUBLICATIONS INDIA

Dedicated
to
Dadima
who told me so many wonderful stories

Contents

Prologue/Epilogue

There are the usual wardens, deans and directors but the chief guest today is this single-decker on six wheels – an engineering marvel – a green missile.

'...Almost every new scientific idea seems preposterous at first...most of us act foolish only to laugh at it...but there are some foolhardy enough to chase the dream and make it a reality...who would have thought that man could fly?'

With that Professor P.P. Sidhu concludes his speech, and adds in his usual cheerful tone, 'Are we ready for the first drive of Bazook 2.0?' He wears a brown check blazer and red turban to celebrate the occasion.

'You may change its name to anything...' I remark to him quietly.

'But it will forever remain good old Biobull for you,' he completes. 'For me too, Tejas. Only the sponsors don't like it...'

It's been a year since we passed out. Foxy, Dusky and I. Tanker, of course, is still at it. He couldn't make it today on account of a re-test.

Meanwhile, a lot has happened. Since the first drive of Bazook 1.0, I mean. Rajit has joined the bus project and stands between mentors – professors Sidhu and Iyer – at the moment. Vineet, my brother, has since returned from the US and is actually with the VC firm that funds version 2.0.

My family is there to enjoy the ride, which includes my parents and nagging, but in the end, helpful sisters – Sneha and Ria didi.

Dr Prabhakar, seen without his stethoscope here, was true to his word and has resumed touch with his friend, my father. He chats with him right now.

Mr Fate's presence is obviously felt, for without his efforts this reunion wouldn't have been possible. I strain my ears to try and discern the sound of his ol' harmonica in the air.

Biobull itself has changed, some will say for good. Give me my bright green garage manufactured companion any day, I'd retort. It's been two years since I first made its acquaintance and in between it has become more like a harpoon and a shade darker. But my fondness remains.

'The story of my life is the story of this bus,' it forces me to remark.

'Not your arbit fundas, again, Tej!' Dusky snubs me.

'How much have you lived anyway?' questions Foxy.

As I watch them all enter the bus ahead of me, though, I am reminded of the story of my life. The story of my journey, anyway.

'I wake up in the morning
To the sound of raindrops,
And I wonder where you'd be,
And I wonder if it's raining there.
Wherever you are, I hope you think of me,
When it's raining there,' I hummed as I got into the bus.

July–October, that year

T he seed of my voyage was planted right here.

Shreya was leaving Delhi for Chennai – that is where she lived, a good two thousand kilometres away from me – after a short vacation. I decided I must see her off at the station. Her mother would be there but I thought I'd manage to get across an utterance or two of my love safely over the babble of the station.

Those were tough times. I had hardly got a chance to have her all by myself over the past week. I hadn't managed to do anything special for her. Which is a thing to do with lovers. Here also I was not alone. Foxy and Dusky had tagged along for they had never met Shreya in person and the whole prospect of bidding her farewell right at the station filled them with emotions their own half-love-stories couldn't provide. Besides, they maintained that their approval of my girl was more important than my own.

Foxy took the *filmi* moment to another level by helping Shreya's mother with her suitcase and depositing them both safely in the coach. Shreya managed to jump out with time to spare and met us behind Wheeler's.

As she bowled over my pals with her charm, I could not help but wonder when I'd see her next. When would she come to Delhi again? The whole business made me sentimental and, finding that I had a pen in my pocket, I excused myself and wrote a two line poem that popped into my head, on the torn end of a newspaper.

Never mind the lines and the passion contained within. As the train took off, I ran after her and pressed the note into her hands.

ॐ

The couplet's story, as you have guessed by now, doesn't end here. In course of time it was discovered by her mother who played a passing-the-parcel and the fading words reached Shreya's father. Who, on discovering lines written by a lover to his daughter addressing her dangerous unmentionables, leapt in the air and hit the ceiling. Which impaired his brain forever.

For him it seems the note was not merely a note, but a ticking time bomb, threatening to blow his daughter up one day. Thus he declared, yes, in those archaic times they had the authority, that his daughter must be kept in the strictest of custodies, with barbed wires and all.

ॐ

My heart beat faster each time Shreya did not answer the phone. Finally she did.

'Where have you been the whole day?'

'Ma and papa were around.'

'The whole day? You couldn't even spare a minute?' I should have tried to understand but my temper took over, 'What a stupid explanation! Our life hasn't exactly been smooth lately. But you never bother!'

'Right. I am never bothered!'

'Is all well?'

'How does it matter? I am not bothered. And you shouldn't be either.'

'Shreya ... All well?' I asked, a little worried.

'I can't talk right now. I'll call you at night. Around eleven-thirty.' Her tone suggested something was wrong.

'You can at least tell me in a word if everything is fine or not!'

'I won't be able to now. Please ...'

'Shreya ... A hint?' I summoned all my guts to say, 'I hope you are coming here in December.'

'No,' she said after a pause, her voice on the verge of breaking down.

I couldn't talk any more. Even though I knew that it was on the cards, I needed some time to absorb the shock.

🌾

Now if you are not as dim as the bulb that struggles to light up my room for want of voltage, you must have gathered the reason behind my voyage. My decision was spontaneous. I had to go there as she was not coming here, because we had to meet. Logic in love is simple. Those who've never been smitten by the bug of love may find it a tad difficult to comprehend it, but if they only lie coolly on a sofa and think about all the movies they have seen, and all the crazy things that lovers often do, the fog will begin to clear up.

I hope you get it. After all, I hadn't resolved to build a palace in my lover's name, and cut the hands of the artists thereafter. Or, for that matter, I was not even writing letters in blood, my own of course. I would merely be undertaking an expedition, harmless but risky all the same.

When you have not met for about six months the one who, as the saying goes, makes your heart beat faster and steals your sleep and peace, you think you'd rather die. It is wise, therefore, to try and do anything that makes the union possible. Hence the journey.

There remained one question. How?

After talking to her, I got my act together and thought about all the possible ways to go to Chennai during the winter vacations. Before analysing each in depth, I decided to call my love. Poor thing, she must have been crying.

'Hi!' I said, behaving as if nothing had happened to the world.

'What happened?' Shreya asked with her innate sweetness.

'Nothing, just wanted to apologise for hanging up like that. I am sorry ...'

'It is fine. I understand.'

'Now, tell me what happened ...'

'Raju bhaiya is getting married ...'

'Raju bhaiya ...' I tried to place him among her numerous cousins, 'The one who used to carry you piggyback all vacation long?'

'He used to sleep in the night ...' she tried her hand at humour.

'I hope you got down before that ...' I asked and she chuckled.

'Yes, and yes, he is the same ...'

'Where is he these days?'

'Pune.'

'Where is the marriage? Pune?'

'No, here in Chennai ...'

'The auspicious date?'

'Likely in December ...'

'Had to be ...'

'When mummy came to know about it, she asked papa if we could visit Delhi in November before the marriage ...' Shreya paused. Her mother's mother lived here.

'Then?'

'Papa told her that she could go to Delhi ...'

'Or hell if she wished so, but "Shreya will stay here with me",' I completed for her.

'He said he was sure I'd deceive them again and meet you!'

'Deceive? As if were planning to rob his bank. You don't worry, I will come.'

'You? Here? Don't be stupid …'

'We'll talk about that at night.'

๛

She called at eleven-forty.

Our infatuation still fresh, we loved to talk into the night. We lost all sense of time and surroundings and became completely lost in each other when, suddenly, one of us saw the watch – been rather long; two hours! A trifle if you take into account the other long twenty-two hours of the day, but absurdly long for an STD call.

'If that's the game,' I told her, 'then I will come to Chennai. I have many options. I told you about my industrial tour in December. I can bunk it ….'

'You must not lie at your home. If you are caught, there'll be more problems. Right now, only my parents know …'

'We'll have to take that risk, Shreya.'

'No!'

The mere thought of travelling across the country to Chennai had dispelled the last trace of gloom in the air. I already looked forward to my adventure. My tone now brimmed with exuberance.

'Shreya, do you want to meet me or not?'

'Of course, I do. But it doesn't look practical …'

I repeated, 'Do you want to meet me or not? Say yes or no and nothing else.'

'Yes.'

'Then, stop crying and stop worrying. I will come, darling. What is life without a dash of thrill,' I said philosophically, 'and, if we pull this off, won't we have nice things to tell our grandchildren?'

'Shut up!'

'It will be ungrateful of us to kick this god-given chance to enjoy life ….' I went on.

'You'll come this far, Tej, just for me?'

And the lovelorn souls went on talking into the night. Things so full of philosophy that are too grand for this book; things so silly that should not be heard outside the lovers' ears.

~

The green lawns of Indian Institute of Technology, Delhi stretched out in delight. The trees smiled, the birds sang, the tall MS (multi-storeyed) building shone, and, lectures over, Dusky, Foxy and I chirruped at the Holistic Food Centre, a cosy mess in IIT.

The month of October is ideal for plotting. The weather invigorates you thoroughly. There is no worry about wiping the sweat off your brow, or about crossing your arms to counter the winter chill. The cool breeze brings with itself fresh ideas, and the feeble sun is warm enough to ripen them. All I had done for the past two days was to stretch out in the sun and let my mind wander and ponder. And now, I discussed the possibilities with two of my comrades.

Said Dusky: 'My vote is for a month-long internship in a Chennai firm. You will be formally excused for the industrial tour then. There'll be no fight.'

Remembering his days at Armed Forces Medical College, Pune, my dad, before dropping me for the first time at the hostel, had remarked, 'Time for your real baptism.' In the days to come most of us, along with a wash of our brains, were given a new name. Pritish Tomar, for outfoxing the seniors during ragging became Lomar *urf* Foxy. Rishabh Khosla, being the last rank admitted to our department, first became Dhakkan, and then, for the zeal he showed in overtaking the top-rankers was perennially rechristened Dusky – an amalgam of Dhakkan and Dassi – ten pointer. In a system where you are rated out of ten, it is hard to do better. I, who had the privilege of having Bajrang 'Tanker' Singh as my Room *Baap* – I inherited his room in my first year – was saved from the hands of other insignificant seniors, and Tanker ensured – I entered his good books when he kicked open my door the very first day to find me playing guitar – that Tejas only turned Tej.

To cut a the long story short, Foxy and I were too adventurous in outlook to not notice each other for long, and both spotted a virtue in Dusky which not many of our colleagues possessed – he readily shared his notes with us. In addition, on scratching Dusky's surface, Foxy discovered a playful heart. He might never get himself into trouble but could imperil his life to get us out of a fix.

'No way, yaar,' I said in response to Dusky, 'My dad knows what a sloth I am. He knows I can't work for a day. One month and that too in Chennai. Too much load, bhai...'

Foxy suddenly erupted, 'Cracked it. Ulti idea, boss. The Inter-IIT sports meet at IIT Madras in December. Perfect, boss, perfect. Seals the deal!'

'You mean I should lie at home that I have been selected?' I asked disapprovingly.

'Why not?'

'I can't.'

Here is an exemplary liar. Alright, I was betraying my parents' trust. But let us be reminded that even the biggest knaves have some scruples. They all draw a line somewhere. Robin Hood never swindled the poor. Billy the Kid never murdered innocent women and children. And Tejas Narula could never hurt his father's pride in him.

Deceiving him, who had blind faith in me, pained me no end. But you do understand, I hope, that your protagonist had no choice. Meeting his love was not possible without keeping his dad in the dark. But what he could do was lie morally. There are things worse than lying about what you did on a one-paisa tour, one of them being a white lie about winning gold in a marathon.

Dusky reiterated, 'I still maintain that you should get an internship there.'

'That's a first-rate excuse for you, *maggu*. Not me!'

'And that is way too boring …' said Foxy tongue-in-cheek, and before I could wring his neck for making my life his plaything, he said in time, 'You don't want to fart about Inter-IIT, you can't intern, then just fake the industrial tour.'

'That's the best chance I have. Only the risks involved are high. If, by any chance, my parents come to know, I'll be dead,' I said.

'But how, boss, how? Why will they doubt you at all? If they don't spot anything fishy, there'll be no fight,' Foxy spoke, excited. I got the point in a flash. You can sell a ton of brass as gold if you have the right look on your face.

'Even if they can't reach you any time and call one of us, we'll tell him that you are busy in some factory; and that we'll ask you to call them …'

I felt I was closer to Shreya already. As Foxy and Dusky fought over my plans, as if it was them who were going, I sat back, withdrawing from the conference and was transported two thousand kilometres across the country – blue sky, blue sea, cool breeze. And there I could see Shreya, with her hair blowing in the air, twenty paces from me in a white dress, angel-like, adorned with the slightest of smiles, waiting for me to wrap her in my arms. Why the white dress? Well, that is none of your business.

'Shhh,' said Dusky suddenly, interrupting my dream 'There comes Pappi ...'

'So?' I asked.

'He is the tour in-charge.'

'Who is in charge, stud-boys? Nice weather for beer and bakar,' came a booming voice from behind.

It was Tanker – the Lord of IIT. Take note, you all; two critical characters have just made your acquaintance. For now though, let us keep aside these men of importance. The air was magical, the mood romantic; and all that came to your protagonist's mind was Shreya.

January, the year before that

January. The month that brings with itself a fresh year. January. The month that brought her.

Now that we've arrived to this point in the narrative where I must unfold before you a most unique episode, I must tell you all, my readers, that I was once a sceptic, a ridiculer of this thing called 'Fate'. You may prefer to call it destiny or kismet or coincidence but since the mentioned episode, I have known this entity as Mr Fate. Though guiding my life since birth and, no doubt, yours, his movements were all but obscure to my eyes, until he chose to show up and how!

Now, lie back, all you lovers and let your mind slip back to that fortunate accident, that ingenious stroke of fortune which enabled you to meet your love. I do not talk about the moment you fell in love; no, I talk about the accident, that singular coincidence, when he or she, not yet your love, bumped into your life.

Now, forgive me, I ask you all to delete that incident, though from it hinges your entire life; it is a scenario you shudder to contemplate, but do it; what remains is pizza without cheese.

So it was that Mr Fate had planned a similar accident for me and had it been absent, no doubt, you would not be reading this book and I would still be a sceptic. But now a believer, as I continue the story, I urge you to become one too in the strange workings of Mr Fate – destiny, kismet, coincidence et al – in whose hands we are mere puppets.

It was the eve of my birthday, I recall distinctly. Vineet, my dearest brother, was here on a vacation from the US. Although a character of significance in this story, my brother has only a guest appearance here and I will talk about him in detail later.

We were planning the morrow after my classes at Ria didi's place when she suggested going to a movie. And, now, I tremble to imagine the scenario if she hadn't. Would someone else have? There are other ifs and buts – the cinema halls could have been different, the show timings ... what not ... That it was meant to be is all that comes to my lips. And so it was that didi uttered:

'Is that Shah Rukh movie out?'

'Yes; it is good, I have heard,' someone said.

'Tej, call Sneha and ask her if she can come tomorrow; it'll be fun if the *bacha*-party can get together,' said didi.

'I'll ask her right away.'

It is time for some introductions. Sneha and Ria are my sisters, and if you are curious about the whole real sister and cousin sister thing, you'd say that Ria didi is my cousin and Sneha the real one. Vineet too, is not the real deal.

I called up Sneha without wasting any time. She had been at odds with me and Vineet because we had spent most of the time loafing around, and not with her at home.

'Hi sis! College over?'

'I just entered home. So enjoying yourself?' she asked with sarcasm.

'Of course, you know I always do ...'

'Blah-blah...And how is your brother finding his tour of India?'

'He's been in Delhi, sis …'

'From the nights he has spent at his home, he could be back in his beloved US and I would give a damn …'

'You mind that?'

'Please, I am enjoying a break from you two. Stay out as long as possible and save my head.'

'But sis, unfortunately we'll have to face each other tomorrow …'

'I know. Can't you postpone your birthday?'

'Allow me to add to your excitement by informing you that the plan for your dear brother's birthday is set. We are catching Shah Rukh's movie tomorrow. We'll pick you up from home …'

'Excuse me. First of all, how did you get into that thick head of yours that you are my dear brother?' she thundered. Her mood was such that she could break my neck and not feel sorry about it. I thanked god I wasn't in her vicinity, 'And excuse me again; I am going for that movie already. But not with you all.'

'Trapped a poor boy finally?' I bantered.

'That is none of your business, but tomorrow I will go with my friends.'

'Isn't that plan a bit ridiculous?' I asked in anger. 'Your stupid friends can wait, sis. It's my birthday. Everybody's coming tomorrow including you. I won't take no for an answer,' I ordered.

'Well, that is what you get, brother. A flat no. And don't you dare call my friends stupid.'

'Alright, you can go with your intellectual friends later. Who can be more important to you than your brother?' I appealed to her emotions.

'My best friend is in town after a long time and I've got to meet her.'

'May I ask which one of your best friends this is now?'

'What do you mean which one of …'

'You change them as frequently as baby's diapers. Have you got yourself a new one again?' I was getting steamed up and decided to take her on.

'Shut up! I am talking about Shreya. My school friend.'

'Oh, the same girl that fled to Chennai?' I cursed Shreya. All of us were going together for a movie after such a long time. And this girl had to ruin the celebration.

'Shut up, and bye,' Sneha raged.

'Fine, goodbye. But take my advice, it's better to be with us than to hang around with pseudo friends.'

'I am going to do exactly the opposite.'

'Fine,' I said, angry but saddened.

'Bye …'

'Arre, wait a second. So we won't book your ticket!'

'Yes, I have mine in my hand.'

'Which theatre and show?'

'Priya. 11a.m. show.'

I jumped out of the sofa on hearing that. We had planned to go for the same show. Which completes the accident. But with Mr Fate's job over, it is a man's duty to do his work and so I did. I tried to recall what Shreya looked like. She was pretty, I remembered faintly.

'Sis. Did you hear a harmonica play?'

'What? Are you hallucinating?'

'Anyway, what luck! We are going for the same show, sis.'

'God! Don't you dare talk to me there. I'd prefer my friends not to know that I have a cauliflower like you for a brother.'

'On the contrary, I can already see your friends drooling!'

'Do you have a mirror around?'

'By the way, how many of you are going?'

'Four of us.'

'Any hot chick?'

'Mind your tongue! Friends of your sister are like your sis …'

'Shh … friends … Is Shreya the one whose picture you showed me last time?'

'Yes.'

'She seems interesting.'

'Don't you get ideas, Tej. If you act smart, I'll kill you. Don't you dare talk to me tomorrow!'

'I will not talk to you, of course. Shreya will do. Don't be bothered.'

'Don't you dare!'

'You know me, sis, I will.'

'Good, make a fool of yourself. Your wish. Besides she has a boyfriend. So no hopes, Romeo.'

'Well, not a worry, they come and go, boyfriends…Yesterday he, tomorrow me, day after I don't care, if she has any. Sounds like a poem! Wow, I can speak in verse, sister.'

'Shut up! I'll warn my friends about you – what a flirt you are.'

'Do that. Bye for now, see you tomorrow.'

'Behave yourself tomorrow.'

'Let us see.'

⟐

'Tej, hurry up!' shouted didi.

'Coming,' I shouted from inside the loo.

'Not even girls take that long to get ready!'

'Just a minute!'

I looked for the hundredth time in the mirror. And set my hair one last time with my hand. Boys like me don't fancy combs. I should have had a haircut last week, I thought, when my mother was after my life and had threatened to chop my mop while I was asleep. I had slept with the door bolted for the entire week. How I wished now that I had listened to her; for once she was right.

She is always too finicky about my hair and its length, and if she has her way, she'd soak my hair in a gallon of oil and comb it back adhered to my scalp, and then proudly introduce me as her '*babu-beta*'. And I, who had grown up admiring the dishevelled mane of Paul McCartney, naturally suffered irreconcilable differences with her on all hair related subjects. But today there was no doubt about it. She was right. God bless the souls who say 'Listen to your mother', I thought. The more I looked, the more I felt like Conan, the famous barbarian. Finally, I gave up shaping the bush into something civilised. I gave a fleeting glance at my visage, which I had forgotten in the wake of the hair crisis. I had three juicy pimples on my nose. 'Bloody hell!' I muttered. What a birthday gift that was! I wondered at the injustice of god, when shouts came from everywhere. I shot out of the bathroom that very instant.

A step out in the sun was just what the doctor would have prescribed for me. As I inhaled the fresh breeze, I could feel my woes fading away and a balmy feeling abounding inside me. I looked up. The sky was blue and there was not a spot to be seen. The whole canvas was lit up by a splendid sun. Just the sort that brightens up your soul on a winter day. It was the kind of morning when a bloke after stepping out in his pyjamas, stretches his arms, yawns and mumbles to himself, 'Ahaaaa'. I did as much. Mine is a mood governed more by the weather than the planets.

The vivacious ambience struck the right chord and sent a signal to the brain which sent a song to my lips. It was no more than a reflex. 'Summer of '69'. Though it was hardly what you'd call a summer, the song suited the spirit. The air resonated and sang along with me. I wished that I could play my guitar. My mind lit up by the prospects of the morning, I moved to the car with a hip and a hop.

Priya was a half-an-hour drive and the *bacha*-party reached well before time. The attendance for the morning show being thin, we spotted Sneha with two friends the moment we reached. Shreya was missing. Sneha wished me in person. Preliminary introductions revealed that the two girls were Saumya and Kamna. Sneha eyed me with the dare-you-flirt look. But I wasn't interested.

'Almost half an hour to go, why don't we all grab a bite?' someone asked. I was too lost to notice.

'Sneha, why don't you join us?' asked didi.

'No, not yet, didi. One of my friends is yet to come. We'll join you once she's here,' Sneha replied.

'Shreya is always late,' complained Saumya or Kamna.

I glanced at my watch. There was about half an hour to go; more if you took into account the advertisements and all. Plenty of time to play around! My mind buoyed by the weather, gave finishing touches to my plan. I excused myself out of the group.

'I am not hungry, didi. I'll flip through some magazines and enjoy the sun for a while.' No one complained. 'Vineet, give me your mobile; didi, give me a call when you are through,' I said.

I didn't own a mobile phone yet. Vineet's phone was of strategic importance as he had acquired a new sim card and no one had his number. I avoided the path where Sneha stood, still waiting. I chose a vantage point and dialled the number. My heart was full of mirth.

'Hullo!' said a sweet voice.

'Hullo!' I changed my voice to a gruff one. 'Is that Sneha?'

'Yes.'

'Beta, I am Shreya's dad. I was stuck at work, so she got late. Sorry for that. She has left with the driver and should reach in ten-fifteen minutes.'

'Oh, namaste uncle! No problem.'

'Namaste beta. That main road leading to the hall is jammed. Please wait at the back entrance.'

'Okay, uncle.'

'And yes, she doesn't have her mobile phone. That's why I called to inform you.'

'Fine, uncle.'

'She doesn't know much about the area and doesn't have a phone.'

'Fine, uncle.'

'Enjoy the movie.'

'Thanks, uncle, we will.'

'Bye.'

'Bye.'

I saw them moving. Going, going, gone. I let out a breath. Job well done. I prayed that Shreya would come soon and not call Sneha on her own. And given the thin crowd, I'd recognise her figure easily.

✣

Standing there, after the successful execution of the first phase of the plan, I started feeling nervous. Girls always give you jitters. It is one thing when you are standing in the sun, rejoicing in your life's calm, when suddenly you sense a slap on your back and, turning, find yourself eye to eye with your childhood crush. But the scale of enormities, when you have told a hundred lies to intercept an unfamiliar beauty, is a unique one. You can still utter, in the first case, life-saving Hi's and Ya's while the mind is holidaying. But the second case is hopeless.

All of my inhibitions assumed the form of a giant demon and punched me in the face. Bang! What a mess I looked! Bad hair, pimples... If there was a market for it, you could have made a fortune by extracting a gallon of juice from them. I began to feel like an idiot. What a foolish plan to devise! The bright sun and the cool breeze gave no respite. I was about to give my plan a serious second thought when lightning struck.

Her majesty appeared. Someone blew into a harmonica.

Well ... Countless books and innumerable movies celebrate with fanfare the arrival of the heroine. Strong winds start to blow, thunderstorms strike and as if this noise was not deafening enough, loud music erupts and the *tapori* in the front row acknowledges it all with a sincere whistle. Poets write lyrics heralding the descent of the divine beauty from heaven. One reads incomprehensible stuff about rosy cheeks, coral lips and starry eyes, entwined with the indecipherable thee(s) and thou(s) and thy(s). I have neither the ability of the poet nor the flourish of the dramatist. How I would have loved to write my own paean but all I could do then was be floored.

To my eyes, the one before me was like a painting. A song. Everything about her was so graceful and fluid. Like breeze, she flowed towards me, her hair flying and silver *jhumkas* dancing. She was the breeze. With a whiff of perfume. Can one ever say if there is love-at-first-sight or not? But, to your hero, the answer was crystal clear.

That moment will remain with me forever, framed and gilded. When I close my eyes, it all comes back to me, and my heart dances with delight; the perfect picture ... her glowing face, her baby nose, her shiny, flying hair, her dangling earrings, her mirror-work bag by her side, her red stole, her blue jeans and her searching eyes.

Shreya looked around for her friends, confused. I had to move before she took her mobile phone out, if she had one. I regained consciousness and composure. There was no use worrying. She'd not eat me; nor was she the last girl on earth. I had to act. Be a man, Tej, I ordered myself. I looked at my clothes again. Not a bad jacket, a US university sweatshirt, naturally faded jeans. 'Be a man!' I said to myself again and walked towards this heavenly creature.

The close-up only enhanced her beauty. Her searching eyes were innocent and dainty. She had a pink complexion, and her red stole made her look all the more radiant. Winters! Girls, they never look better. Despite the woollens, I could see that she had a lissom figure. She was simple. And beautiful. Perfect.

I gave her a slight pat on her shoulder from the side. She turned towards me, drowning me in her sweet scent. And I was lost in her brown eyes. Magic! She had a hint of kajal in her eyes.

'Yes?' she asked, breaking the spell. 'Talk, idiot!' I said to myself.

'Shreya?' I asked.

'Yes,' she said surprised, obviously.

'Hi! I am Sneha's brother,' I said and put forward my hand. She took it in her soft hands. She smiled and returned the greeting. There was a hint of gloss on her chiselled lips. Extremely kissable. I ventured into solving the puzzle for her straightaway.

'No doubt you are surprised. Don't be. Sneha will be here soon. Actually one of your friends, Saumya, I suppose, has lost her way. Sneha has gone to fetch her with the driver. I had come to drop her but your friend thought it better that I stay and keep you engaged till she comes back. So here I am.' God, I speak too much, I said to myself.

'Well, thanks!' Shreya flashed her smile again. She didn't say anything else. Why don't these girls speak?

'I am Tej, by the way. Hi again. I hope this was a better introduction.' I had availed another opportunity to shake her hand.

'So, how much time will she take?' Shreya inquired.

'Not much, I guess.' What to talk about, I thought. 'So, how is Chennai?'

'Well, not bad. But, nothing like Delhi.'

'Absolutely! Nothing beats Delhi. Winter will be a pleasant change, I suppose, from boiling Chennai.'

'Yes, a lot better. It is really hot there.'

'And really cold here. I think a cup of tea is welcome.'

'Okay.'

'What about you? Tea? Now don't be formal and all.' I thought I said that like an aunty.

'No, I prefer coffee.'

'Oh, wow! Me, too. Let us have coffee then.' I hated coffee. I took her to a corner so that we were not visible. I bought two cups of coffee and furthered the conversation.

'So you graduate next year? Sneha talks a lot about you.' The question was calculated to generate an inquiry about my prestigious college. It worked.

'Yes, I am. What do you do?'

'Well, I am studying industrial engineering.'

'From?'

'IIT Delhi,' I announced grandly. I hoped to see an open mouth or a twinkle in her eye but there was nothing. Again, just her lovely smile. I was running out of topics and time now. She was not helping either with just her monosyllables and smiles. I hadn't expected her to be gregarious the first time but hadn't bargained for such reticence either.

'So it must be difficult … leaving friends here and settling in a new city.'

'Yes, initially; but it's better now.'

'Yes, one has to adjust.' I just couldn't give up the aunty tone. 'I saw some of the snaps you sent to Sneha the other day. You looked nice.' That was as subtle as I could get.

'Thanks!'

And there was a major breakdown again. I began to feel self-conscious. You strain every part of your brain to search for a topic, yet you find none. It is like nothing interesting exists in the whole damned world.

'Just about fifteen minutes left. Let us have a look at some books in the meanwhile. You like reading?' she asked and proceeded towards the corner book stall.

'Oh yes, nothing like books! So who's your favourite author?'

'Well, no favourite as such. I haven't read that many books. But yes, I like John Grisham and Eric Segal.'

'Love Story …' I immediately said, knowing that most girls loved it. I had read almost all Segal books. I hadn't read any Grisham.

'Yes, it was amazing. In fact, that's the only one I have read of Segal.'

'You must read Doctors.'

'So, who's your favourite author?' she asked, picking up a Grisham novel. The Firm.

'Well, I love R.K. Narayan. Have read all of his books.'

'I guess I have read one of his too, Coolie.'

'No, that's by Mulk Raj Anand,' I said politely, trying not to be condescending, yet being impressive.

'Oops. You are right. But yes, I've seen the complete Malgudi Days on TV. I loved that.'

'Same here. That remains my favourite. So real and subtle! And nowadays, you have these mindless soaps. Those were the days …' I sounded like an octogenarian, I thought.

'I think I should buy this one. I'd like to read more of Grisham.'

'Right. After all he is your favourite author,' I said teasingly, 'Like Segal, I bet you have read only one of his too.'

'No, actually two,' she burst out laughing. And so did I. It seemed that we had struck a chord now. The topics came up naturally. She shed her indifference. There were just ten minutes to go. She bought the book and I bought one too, of Wodehouse. For a memorable moment, we teamed together to haggle for books.

She told me she loved to dance. I told her that I was hopeless at it. But I appreciated music. 'By the way, I can strum a string or two.'

'Fundoolicious!'

'What was that?'

'Oh, it's a word we use in college. I'd like to hear you play sometime.'

'I think I will grant you the privilege,' I said, knowing the privilege would be mine.

'I am honoured.'

'So, when do you leave? I'll try and fix an appointment.'

'I am sorry, Tej, I leave tomorrow. Next time, perhaps.'

'No problem, but in return you must teach me how to dance.'

'Only if you teach me how to play the guitar ...'

'Deal.'

'Deal.'

We shook hands again. I would feel their softness for days to come. Learning dance from that angel! I was lost in dreams. How could such a pretty girl be so affectionate with an imbecile like me! My reverie was broken when I heard her say excitedly, 'Hi Sneha!'

ᴥ

All I could manage to say in a few broken sentences was this:

'Hi ... Sneha ... So you ... are back ... good ... This is Shreya, by the way ... A good friend ... I guess you two know each other ... Shreya ... This is my dearest sister ... Sneha.' I was dead.

'Hi Shreya!' Sneha said, smiling at her. Then she turned towards me. 'By the way, she is my friend.'

'Oh! What a coincidence. I could never have thought that we'd have a common friend.' Saumya and Kamna intervened saying a lengthy 'Hi' each and asked Shreya what she was doing here at the entrance when she was supposed to be there at the back.

'What!' Shreya uttered, surprised.

'Yes, your dad called and said that you'd arrive at the back entrance. But after waiting, we came back here to check again,' explained Sneha.

'My dad? Sneha, he left yesterday. How could he have called?' asked Shreya, surprised again.

Well, the director of the scene would have wanted to me to quit the stage, now, and I itched to do the same. 'Sounds like a confusion to me. The movie is going to start soon. I better go. You should also hurry up or you'll miss the beginning,' I said and looked at Shreya.

'Yes, we should move. Nice meeting you, Tej.'

'The pleasure is all mine, Shreya. And don't you forget our deal.'

'Well, you are the one who is busy. I hope I get an appointment,' she said, teasing.

'Oh, I am always free for pretty girls. Bye.'

I shook her soft hand again for the fourth time. I wondered when I'd hold her hand again. I hadn't the slightest clue that it would be so long. I looked at Sneha. She gave me a dreadful look. I smiled at her too. One of those I-won-you-lost smiles. Saumya and Kamna looked disgusted. They turned and moved away. I faintly heard Shreya asking them,

'So, Saumya, where were you stuck?' They proceeded and I watched her go. Her hair and earrings and figure. I longed for her.

As they went farther, I noticed some unrest. I could not make out their conversation but assumed it centred round me and my antics. Their battalion suddenly stopped and turned around. It was not unlike the synchronous about-turn of the jawans on Republic

Day. And 'about-turn' I did and started walking in the opposite direction, when Sneha called out, 'Tej, just a minute.'

'Yes,' I said, turning around. They were right in front of me. Four of them. All furious. Right then I heard didi call out my name. Her battalion marched towards us. I had been cornered, and how! It must be a trying experience for the Mafioso, I thought, the moment of entrapment. All those ingenious plots they must have devised, the dangerous plans they must have executed ... the joy they must have derived from their successes ... must have all dissolved and disappeared in a flash, in this moment of truth. I could sympathise with them.

'Sneha, let them go and watch the movie. I'll explain everything to you,' I said coolly.

'Oh! Don't be afraid, Tej. Let everyone learn about your glorious deed.' She was boiling.

'I'll take a minute to explain. Let them go. Don't create a scene here.'

I told didi that I'd come in a minute. She teased me: 'Flirting around, Mr Tejas?'

I smiled and said, 'I am glad you understand, didi.' I gave back the mobile phone and took my ticket.

Vineet whispered to me, 'You rascal, mend your ways. I'll kick your butt when you come back.'

I returned to the furious four.

'What did you tell Shreya?' Sneha got ready for the court martial.

'I saw you leaving this place. So I assumed Shreya was not coming for the movie. But when I saw her here, I thought I might as well talk to her a little and then tell her to join you. It was harmless, sis.'

'Come to the point, Mr Tejas. What about the phone call?'

'Which phone call?'

'It can't be a coincidence that we are asked to go at the back while you flirt at the front.'

'Excuse me. I didn't flirt. Ask Shreya. I merely talked to her.'

Shreya was puzzled. She didn't know what to say. The look in her eyes at that moment couldn't be described as amiable. Sneha moved away and did something with her mobile phone. She dialled Shreya's dad's number, I guess. A series of awkward expressions followed. She came back as red as a tomato and shouted, 'That was Vineet's mobile.'

'Which mobile?' I asked innocently.

'From which Shreya's dad called.'

'But how did Shreya's dad get hold of his mobile? Do they know each other? Small place, this world, extremely!'

'Stop your nonsense, I mean *someone* used his mobile acting like Shreya's dad!'

'Oh my god, I can't see why Vineet would do that. Something's fishy...'

'Tej, stop fooling us. I can't believe you did that,' she said, looking hurt. 'I am sorry, Shreya. I didn't know he was capable of such a disgraceful thing.' My heart winced at hearing the word 'disgraceful'. Some words are like pocket bombs. My sister was hurt.

'It is okay, Sneha. Don't feel bad. You didn't do anything,' said my darling, comforting her. She was not even looking at me. I moved towards my dear sister. 'I am sorry, sis. I didn't realise you'd feel so bad. Honestly, I did all this just to get even with you.

'Tej, you have crossed all the limits this time ...'

'Sneha, I didn't feel good that you were going out with your friends on my birthday. I am sorry. I went too far ...'

I lied. Of course, I wanted to flirt with Shreya. But I had to lie. She was seriously hurt. I took Sneha's hands in mine and said sorry again. I meant that, though. 'Now, please don't spoil my birthday, sis.

Cheer up. The movie is about to start. You haven't missed anything. First fifteen minutes are ads.'

Saumya and Kamna looked away in disgust. Shreya looked at me, without any anger, I guess. Then she said to Sneha. 'It is okay *na*, dear. Honestly, I didn't feel bad. So please don't fight with him, and cheer up. And yes, his behaviour was fine.' She was sweet.

'I am sorry, Shreya. Can I talk to you for a moment? In private,' I dared to ask her. She nodded.

We moved away. Rest of them proceeded towards the hall. 'I am sorry,' I said looking into her pretty eyes.

'It's okay. You are quite a prankster.'

'Yes. But today it turned out to be horrible. Generally, I tend to make people happy.'

'Oh?'

'Well, I know you won't agree. I am really sorry if I hurt you. But it was really nice meeting you. And I mean that.'

'Fine. But, honestly, I don't like boys who are after girls like this.' An acidic comment.

'Please! I am not after you,' I said, trying to be polite. 'I am sorry if I gave you any such impression. I just tried to be a little friendly; it turns out I already have spoiled the day for so many people,' I said, trying to gain sympathy.

She softened.

'It's okay, Tej. Just be a little careful ...' We started walking towards the hall.

'And yes, please pep up my sis. I know you will do that. And you can tell her that I was decent with you; that'll help.'

'Fine. I will do that,' she said. She had been so considerate and composed during the whole episode. 'Interesting meeting you anyway.' She smiled after a long time. That brightened me up. I felt it had turned out brilliantly.

'Bang on, miss! It is always fun ... being with me. I feel life should be a little adventurous. Normal is boring. What do you say?'

'I have a rather weak heart.'

We reached the entrance of the theatre. I glanced at my watch. We were about twenty minutes late. We stopped before going in.

'Don't worry, ma'am, you wouldn't have missed much. The movie has just started,' I said, putting on some sophisticated charm.

'I am not worrying, I have already seen it. It is you who should worry, sir.' And she laughed. She was not very displeased with the developments, I supposed.

'Oops,' I uttered, laughing, 'We better rush in then. A moment more though, ma'am. What happens to the guitar and dance lessons? Are they still on?'

'I can't say, right now. I'll have to think about it, sir,' she said playing around. That killed me.

'Do tell me though. I hope to stay in touch. Shall I give you my email ID?'

'Your wish.'

I took that as a yes and gave her mine. And got hers too. Fundoolicious, Tej, fundoolicious, I said to myself. We moved in, finally. I hardly cared about the movie.

'By the way, happy birthday.'

'Thanks, don't I get a gift?'

'No,' she said just like a girl can. We finally parted.

This was the unique episode, then, my readers, an impeccable work of Mr Fate. I sang as I marched towards my seat.

Happy Birthday to you!
Happy Birthday to you!

> *Happy Birthday, dear T-e-j-a-a-a-s,*
> *H-a-p-p-y B-i-r-t-h-d-a-y, t-o y-o-u-u-u-u-u!!!!*

I distinctly remember, even though spellbound, that as I sang I heard a harmonica play along.

September, the year before that

'So tell the tale, Mr Romeo.'

'Right away, didi, right away.'

Ria didi is my confidante and agony aunt. It was time for the case to be handled by a more able brain. We walked around the ruins of Jamali Kamali near Qutab Minar, which she maintains, never fails to stimulate her. And I needed her in top form. What would a brother be without his sisters!

'Now will you tell me her name?'

'Shreya Bhargava.'

'Wow,' she laughed. 'Won't you add her dad's name too? I am not asking you for the name of the seventeenth president of Mozambique, idiot. Just say Shreya, dumbo,' she continued to laugh.

'Yes, so Shreya she is.'

'Now wait a minute … Shreya, did you say?' It all came back to her as it must to one with a detective's eye. 'The same girl you embarrassed at Priya …'

'Come on, didi, I did not …'

'You did it then,' she said shaking her head. 'You finally managed to win a girl's heart. A rather pretty girl's heart…'

'You feel the same then, do you?' I said, forlorn.

'What do I feel?'

'Ah!'

'Who else feels the same?' she whispered and I smiled.

'I.'

'And what do you feel, Tej?'

'That she is too good for me.'

'Ah! Looking for an ego massage? Why don't you shoot to the nub of the matter?' asked the expert.

'She lives some two thousand kilometres away,' I said plainly.

'So? Do you love her or not?'

I saw she needed to be fed the complications of the story but for the moment I just replied, 'I do. I think I do.'

'Look at you blush, brother. Wait a minute, does she?' One could see the air had not failed to work its magic.

'Fundoolicious!' I exclaimed out loud.

'What was that?' didi asked.

'It's a word we use in college. Just appreciating your methods.'

'So?' she asked me, not deviating from the topic.

'That's another problem,' I attempted to summarise, and hoped the understatement would produce the effect. 'So, one, Shreya is so far away. Don't know when we'll meet if at all we do. Two, I am not sure she likes me.'

'Do you two talk, umm, romance?' she asked, chuckling. I could see through her methods now. Patient dissection of the facts. She was a handbook on the steps to love.

I delivered the speech I had rehearsed as part of case preparation. 'Didi, my intention was never to woo her. True, I loved her the first time I saw her. But then the distance became a big deterrent. I thought about her a lot initially but then came back to earth. It is great to be friends with her. We gel so well. I like it this way.'

'So ... now, the distance has reduced or what?'

'Well, I have been thinking ...' In fact, that had been the only thing on my mind. 'She comes here about twice a year. So ...

sometimes I feel … I like her so much and can wait for her, but at other times I feel it may prove to be a bit too much.'

'Too much, as in, sir?'

I had chosen lofty words for part two of the declamation. 'As in, didi, my college years are running past me and I haven't even dated a girl. Isn't it distressing, didi? Sometimes I feel like a terminally ill man, with just two years of life left who wants to make the most of them. Hence the quick need for a girl who is nearby. It is a race against time.'

I wonder, now, how immature and foolish I was to say all that. How ignorant I was of love – of its meaning and power. Still, I mention it in the hope that some of you will learn from what my didi said in response.

'Race against time! My foot! What do you want, brother; a timepass?'

'Isn't it rotten to leave a girl once you are done?'

'Glad to hear that, brother …'

'But didi … sometimes out of frustration … I do feel … what the heck! Why waste all these years? If that's the only solution, so be it.'

'What if someone does that with me or Sneha?'

Well, what could I say to that? The very question had kept me in check for so long.

'I'd kill that bastard, didi. Sorry for the profanity.'

'Now, what do you say?'

'Well, didi, I would never try to fool around with a nice girl. But these days you do find girls who want no commitment...'

'You don't mean you'll pay for it?'

'Of course, not, didi!'

'Oh, good. Never the one to forget ethics. You mean, a cultured girl who wants to enjoy life…'

'You got it, didi ...'

She slapped me.

'You were right when you said she's too good for you. Time is not running past. Use your head. Wait for her. But only if you love her.'

I nodded appreciatively as she said: 'So, I hope to have cleared all your doubts.'

'Yes, didi. But ...'

'You have to wait for every good thing in life, child.'

'But I don't even know her feelings for me.'

'Leave that for the moment. First tell me, do you love her or not.'

'Well, didi ... All I can say is that I haven't met a better girl. I like her very much and think I love her too,' I said like a child.

'So, idiot, forget about other girls.'

'And what about ... her liking me?'

'That's no IIT entrance problem. Ask her.'

'What!'

'Yes, ask her. There's no point living in doubt. Ask her if she likes you or not.'

'What if she says no?'

'She won't say no outright. She'll just say she never thought about you that way.'

'Whatever, but that means no.'

'That doesn't mean no, brother. That also doesn't mean she has never thought about you that way. That just means she is not that sure about you right now. We'll deal with that later, it won't be that bad. But you have to ask. Show some courage.'

'But didi ... she is very pretty and I ...'

'You are smart, you idiot.'

'Are you serious, didi? Can she like me? What about these pimples?'

'All I can say is, if I were the girl, I would never have said no.'

☙

Bringing back to mind my mishap-ridden journey from childhood, I can fairly accurately say that save for an occasion when, still in half-pants, my molar had gone bad and had to be removed, courage has never failed me. I confess I have never been in the vicinity of a lion or within a gunshot, but I ask you all, are these the only tests of luck? Where my humble life has tested me, I have stood firm, and that brings me gratification.

Yet I tottered when the moment of truth arrived and pleaded with my didi to change her mind. I grumbled a whole day but, 'Be a man!' didi said in the end and that was that. It is compact dialogues like these, these pocket bombs, which, when delivered by army generals to shaky soldiers, change their fortunes forever. They march on to the battlefront.

As for us, we tip-toed to the roof, quietly opening the creaking doors on the way. The night sky was clear, stars were twinkling and the air was refreshing. I have already mentioned numerous times the virtues of pleasant weather. The scented air worked on me like a bottle of spirit.

Didi dialled the number and pressed the phone against my ear. I turned my face away from her. Ring. I started feeling weak on my knees, and that strange sensation in the stomach which one feels when exam scripts are handed, surfaced.

Shreya picked up. 'Hullo,' she said sleepily.

'Hi! Hope you were not asleep.' Of course, she was.

'I was!'

'Never mind … I wanted to … talk to you,' I said slowly.

'Alright! What is it in the middle of the night?'

'I was thinking about us.'

'About us?'

I was at a loss for words. But there was only one way. I had to say it right away. It was unbearable to beat about the bush.

'Shreya, what do you think about me?'

'What sort of question is that, and at this hour?' she asked. I was nervous now. I was certain she'd say, 'I don't like you.' It was better not knowing her thoughts about me.

'I mean, do you like me?'

She didn't say anything for what seemed like an eternity. She was shocked, no doubt, by such an idiotic question. We had been great friends and now that was off too. It was all ruined. She finally said with carefully chosen words.

'See, Tej, I really like you. But as a friend.'

There was silence again.

'I thought I'd tell you my feelings. I really like you.'

'But I have never thought of you that way, Tej.'

Finally the dreaded words that didi had spoken arrived, verbatim, 'I have never thought of you that way.' It irritated me to no end. I wanted to ask her, 'Why on earth haven't you thought of me that way? Am I that bad? I thought we got along really well and shared chemistry. What more do you want? All you girls know is how to trick guys.' I wisely skipped that part.

'Tej, I can't say anything right now.'

I felt didi's hand on my shoulder. I looked into her eyes. No, I didn't blame her for rushing me into this. Good that I got to know about her feelings. I looked at the sky. The stars still sparkled. The world had not changed. I changed my tone to a more cheery one and asked her, 'I hope the door is not closed for me?'

'See Tej, let us continue to be friends and see how things move on.'

'But please keep that door slightly ajar.'

'It is!'

'By the way I have a habit of sneaking in from the windows. Good night!'

'Good night!'

I hung up. Didi took my hands in hers.

'She didn't close the door?'

'No,' I smiled. One of those pensive ones.

'Don't you worry, she needs more time. She has to be sure before she commits. She is a good girl.'

'Can we stay here and talk? The weather is not bad!'

'Sure, brother.'

January, that year

It was ten past three now. Every minute she delayed added to the agony. You want to do away with these things quickly; you do not want to wait at a doctor's clinic knowing beforehand that a syringe is going to drill your butt.

Her words kept echoing in my ears. I wouldn't take 'I haven't thought of you that way' this time. No sir, I wouldn't. She'd have to be clear as crystal. No diplomatic dilly-dallying this time around! For heaven's sake, 'the bell must have rung', as the romanticists say, by now, if there existed one. I had violins playing havoc in my mind! Tell me Shreya, if I am not the one.

I was afraid too. A refusal this time could well mean the end of my innings. And I knew I could never be 'just her friend'.

Finally mademoiselle called. I got myself together.

'Late again!'

'Sorry, but dad called up. So … what were you doing?'

'Nothing, just came down to the park so that I could talk with you freely. To be more specific, I was staring at grass.'

'Alright! Are there no girls today?'

'People prefer to stay indoors at this lethargic time of the day.'

'Sad!'

'Not at all, sometimes I prefer to be in solitude with nature.'

'Sorry for disturbing you, sir.'

'It's okay. Shreya, I want to talk to you about something,'

'Oh my god! What is it now?'

'I don't know if I am rushing into this or not, but it's important to clear some things.'

'Like?'

'You know like what, Shreya.'

'Still, tell me,' she said slowly.

It was tough to say that again. 'About your feelings for me, Shreya.'

I closed my eyes and tried to cool down. 'There are other girls,' I said to myself. 'But can there be anyone like her?'

'What do you think, Tej?'

'Let us not fool around, Shreya.'

'You are a very good friend, Tej … and I don't want to lose you.'

'I get it, Shreya. I won't ever ask you again …'

'Let me first finish what I have to say. Will you promise me something?'

'What?'

'Will you remain as good a friend always?'

There was a lump in my throat. I was angry with myself for being so sentimental.

'Promise me!'

'I promise. Bye for now,' I managed to say and a tear slipped down my cheek.

'Wait! Promise me another thing.'

'What?' I asked, trying to sound normal.

'Promise me you will remain a friend even if I tell you that I love you.'

I don't know how to put my feelings in words. It was like a sudden shower on an oppressing day. I did not smile for I wanted to be sure.

'What?'

'I love you, Tej!'

'I love you, too,' I repeated stupidly.

'I know that.'

I wiped my eyes and indulged in a smile. An ever so small one.

'So why didn't you tell me?'

'Boys ask first, dumbo.'

'But I did, last time.'

'I wasn't sure then, but now that I was, I wanted you to ask me.'

'I hope I understand your species some day.'

'Best of luck!' She giggled.

'Will you tell me what made you decide on me this time? I'll try and remove the misconceptions.'

'Shut up! You still haven't made the promise.'

'Oh! I'll think about it.'

'What do you mean you'll think about it?'

'I mean … it takes time to decide on these emotional matters. Who knows better than you, Your Highness?'

It was nice to be on top, for once.

~

I dialled her number next.

'Hi Didi …'

I had to tell her.

Back to October, that year

So we are back here again after that little interval of nostalgia, and, though my heart yearns for more of it, we must move ahead. I had decided, more or less, that I'd skip the industrial tour. I waited for the tour dates to be announced, and one fine afternoon, having enjoyed my siesta in Pappi's 'Alternate Fuel' lecture, I woke up to Dusky's voice. He was our Class Rep and had his hands up, valiantly attempting to control the menacing class.

'Yes, I will announce the dates if you will all allow me to.'

'Who the hell has gagged you?'

'Okay … We leave Delhi on the 10th. Reach Pune on the 11th. Leave for Goa on the 17th and start back for Delhi on the 20th. We'll return on the 22nd.'

'Only three days in Goa! Damn the tour!'

The whole class broke into a clamour. Groups of friends discussed among themselves what they'd do on the tour. Some darted weird questions at Dusky, who, being polite in demeanour, could never satisfy the rascals. A friend shouted, 'Why don't we leave for Goa earlier?' And then suddenly the whole class invented a slogan: 'We want Goa! We want Goa!'

For the first time I felt like an outsider. I wasn't party to their joy. I moved out quietly and no one noticed. They were lost in celebration. Now that I knew the tour dates, I could finalise my plan.

I felt a pat on my shoulder. It was Dusky.

'Are you sure you'll bunk it?'

I nodded. 'I will miss you all,' I smiled and said.

'What'll Foxy do without his partner in crime?'

'It's time you graduate, Dusky,' I said and shook his hand.

'She is a nice girl, Tej. Make sure you are careful.'

ᴥ

I produce here, as an exhibit, the original specimen of my modus operandi. I would, no doubt, have loved to share with you the detailed discussions it required, but to make the novel lighter, we must avoid them.

1. **Departure**: *10th December, to Pune, Goa Express, with the rest of the class – a simple precaution against the traditional habit of the Indian family to see off its children at the station*

2. **Arrival**: *Pune, 11th evening; call on dad's mobile from landline showing Pune's code – thereafter every call from my mobile – location concealed.*

3. **While in Pune**: *Click as many photographs, changing clothes as many times, at as many landmarks, changing the date fed in the camera each time – Visit – AFMC College, dad's alma mater, and Kayani Bakery to buy Shrewsberry biscuits for home.*

4. **Departure**: *11th midnight, to Chennai, Chennai Express.*

5. **Arrival**: *Chennai, 8 PM, 12th, 10 days stay.*

6. **While in Chennai**: *Call home at least twice everyday – give them no reason to call – keep in touch with friends for their whereabouts in Pune/Goa.*

7. **Return Strategy**: *Industrial tour ends on 20th – too few days with Shreya – inform home that Foxy, Dusky and I, are staying back to enjoy Goa for three more days – Parents expect me back on 25th,*

instead I return on 24th – eliminating any possibility of them receiving me at the station – station problem at both ends solved.

I distinctly remember the thrill and satisfaction I experienced each time I went over the document. I was about to travel the length of the country. I could hear the whistle of the engine. The wheels were about to roll.

✍

All the planning done, and, now, within an ace of action, I must tell you that although it all looks very easy, to my mind it was not. For days I lived in the fear of being caught by my parents. Though they are pretty understanding otherwise, I was certain they'd feel let down should my plan fail. My mind, disturbed by negative thoughts, was helped in no way by my friends and kin in whom I confided, for they admitted frankly that they wouldn't have done it. And they were right too. After all, I was bunking a compulsory educational tour – lying to professors – spanning the country to meet a girl – all of it while keeping my parents in dark. I shuddered to contemplate all of it coming out in the open together.

How, then, did I steel myself? True, I was madly in love and compelled by the drive only a lover knows. Yet, an incident from childhood played no small part in strengthening my resolve.

Once during my exams in high school, I was caught with two answer sheets – one of them mine, of course, diligently copying a complex solution. There was a huge scandal. The teachers, one can still understand, treated me like the rotten fish that spoils the whole pond, but even my peers, who might not have been entirely scrupulous in their ways, looked down upon me.

Therefore you can imagine the state of my heart when I told my father about the summon orders. I felt that I was a stain on the blemish-less lineage. I expected a thrashing and closed my eyes in anticipation when I heard my father say 'You should always be careful, son!'

I prayed that he'd relate to my present mischief in some way and be accommodating. He told me, only years later, about his own sheet-swapping exploits, and I hoped there was something in his closet, some wild act, about which I was unaware till now.

Professor Pappi and I

Professor Prabjot Pal Sidhu, of the Mechanical Engineering Department, Indian Institute of Technology, Delhi, was a man noted for an exceptionally unruffled demeanour. His wife noted it the very first night of their marriage, and his peers, the day he joined. His students noted it before the lecture started, which is never a good thing. But that is not to say that he was not respected.

You'd describe him as a Sardar of short stature if you only measured him with an inchie tape, for in eminence, every other professor in the country followed him. If the bus that carried the students to and fro between the hostel and the institute, and would, in time, carry the whole of Delhi's populace, did not carry his name, it was only a mark of his humility. The CNG engine that ran it was Professor P.P. Sidhu's baby and the word was that he hadn't stopped there.

The aspect of his character that concerns us at the moment is not his scientific competence but his calmness. It showed on his face, which not only meant no harm, but never did any.

'Has he *never* failed a student?' I asked Tanker, who was the last word on professors.

'No, not even me.' Which was a big thing in favour of the argument. 'You dress up Pappi with a kirpan and all and he'd stay the same old Pappi.'

Professor P.P. Sidhu, popular as Pappi among the students, was also, by an act of Providence, the head of the Industrial Tour Committee, to whom one must report in case one wishes to exempt himself from the compulsory tour. And so, it was required that I meet him.

He taught us the fuels course in which I was supposed to make a 'Pneumatic Linear Double Sided Anti-Rotation Tubeless Air Transfer Cylinder', whatever that means. This was to be installed in a breakthrough bus being developed by my institute, which was to run on bio-gas, and I hadn't even gone so far as to decipher the meaning of each term in the title of my project.

This had not impressed Pappi, who, however jovial he might be on the subject of bally tours, was somewhat professional on the subject of projects. I tried telling him mildly that if making cylinders with such obnoxious names were child's play, India's knack for producing such buses would match the one she had for making babies, to which he replied, 'That's exactly where I want to take India.' I had skilfully delayed the project so far, but, now that the semester was coming to an end, the going would be tough.

I saw him bending over a fat book, scribbling down notes with the enthusiasm of a child who has just been gifted his first box of crayons. He looked up at me for a fleeting second and bent down again.

'Sir,' I began, 'I am afraid it won't be possible for me to go on the industrial tour.'

'Ok-a-a-y,' he said in the sort of tone which comes out when one has cold. In his case the cold was perennial.

I didn't know what to do with this long 'Okay'. It couldn't have meant: 'Don't be afraid, son, I am sure whatever prevents you must be a worthy cause.' I endeavoured to speak again, this time clearing my throat. 'Sir, I want to tell you that it is not possible for me to go on the industrial tour.'

'Okay,' he said again as he continued to play with his crayons. The second nasal 'Okay' was a tad too much. What on earth was that supposed to mean? I felt that I spoke to a parrot that had been taught to speak well, the only problem being that the classes had gone only so far as one word. I looked on while he played on. What else can a student do in front of his professor, however jovial he might be, who has in his hands power which can be misused to stop the student from meeting his darling?

It would, no doubt, be astonishing for you all, this parrot-like conduct of the professor, but I knew better. The one adjective that immediately comes to mind, the moment one talks about professors, however rare that might be, is absent-minded. No other adjective could describe our specimen better. Pappi was known to immerse himself some ten thousand leagues under the sea when in the midst of his research, so that it took him an era to come up to sea-level. Presently, I waited for that moment. But then I feared, perhaps he might have drowned. Thus, like a nimble lifeguard, I shot, this time coughing more and speaking louder, 'Sir, does that mean I have got your permission?'

'Yes!' he shouted ecstatically and my insides jumped with ecstasy too. I scarcely believed my good fortune. I admired the professor and his ways, what joy he showed – as if he was handing me his daughter's wedding card! Just when I was about to thank him, he shot out from his seat as if a pin had poked him and shouted, 'Yes, yes, yes!' and looked at me. I wondered what the next three yes's were about, when he ran up to me as euphoric as Archimedes must have been once out of his bath and said, 'Tell me, what's five multiplied by six!'

One doesn't expect that. I wondered if it was a test one had to undergo to secure permission, and I promptly replied thirty to which he said, 'Thirty it is indeed then, you know what! We'll soon have a bus that runs on gas made from human waste, and gives an average of thirty kilometres per cubic ...'

'Congratulations, sir,' I hastened to add.

'Listen! You wait right here and I'll be back!'

Presently he entered with a pile of books and asked me, 'What brings you here?'

'Sir?' I said, hardly believing that he had not heard a thing.

'What sir?'

'Sir, I told you that it is not possible for me to go on the tour.'

'Tour? Ah yes, the tour, indeed, yes, yes, the tour, indeed. Okay!'

'Yes sir! I asked for permission and you said yes.'

'Did I? Okay! But why? What happened? Why are you not going on the tour? It is a privilege to go, isn't it?'

'Sir, it is my brother's marriage.'

'So?'

'Sir, I must attend that!'

'Ah, yes, okay okay, I see, but you'll miss something; it'll be a landmark tour; not just for India but for the world. The first drive of Biobull!'

'Sir, Biobull?'

'Yes, Biobull ... isn't it a wonderful name for my bus?'

'Sir, bus?'

'What else?'

'Sir, the tour, the industrial tour to Pune this winter.'

'Oh, that!'

'Yes sir!'

'You should have told me before.'

'Sir, I did!'

'Okay, okay,' his okays were driving me mad, 'I must have been occupied; you'll be required to write an application which will require my signature. Now go on, please go on.'

'Yes sir!'

'No, wait!'

'Yes sir!'

'Congratulations!'

'Sir?'

'Your brother's marriage!'

'Oh yes, thank you, sir, I'll write the application. Thank you, sir.'

And with that I left his room. I gave him the application later. He said, gleefully, that he would consider it and I could meet him the next day.

How I wish, now, to go back in time and stop the clock here, right here!

🐾

I remember telling Foxy, in his hostel room, about what a gem Pappi was, when a foot banged at the door and the weak bolt, not able to bear the shock, went flying in the air; and flying in came a colossus, evidently drunk, shouting, 'Hello stud-boys!'

It was Tanker. You have met him before but, no doubt, forgotten about it. However, a moment's wait will make such a thing impossible. His parents had named him Bajrang, respectfully after Hanumanji, the most widely worshipped Indian god, in the innocent hope that the name would bless him with a virtue or two of the powerful god. He had acquired none save the size. He was as big as a bull, and when drunk, which he often was, as mad as one. In our circles and many a circle before us, he was called 'Tanker', for his capacity for any form of ethanol.

Foxy called him names, obviously jolted from having his door permanently dis-bolted, and told him not to scream. 'Okay, no fight, brother, I will not shout,' bellowed Bajrang, 'Anything for you, stud-boys. You both are gems, love you both, ask for anything and it will be yours, just ask!' It was said that he spoke from his heart when drunk. Thus the stuff about us two being gems must be true. As you already know, he was my *room-baap* and had ever since looked upon me and my friends as little brothers who must be protected and showered with affection.

'I will certainly tell you whenever I need anything; any special reason behind today's *daru* party?'

'As if they need a reason!' said Foxy.

'Shut up, you sonovabitch! It is Chaapu's treat; he got a job with ITC,' he said totally out of his senses, 'And you both are coming with me. He has called you both; have a bit of beer, a bit of *bakar*; we have ordered pizzas. Come, come, and, Tej bhai, get your guitar.' *Bakar*, by the way, is directionless talk.

Today I was in too good a mood to refuse.

'Come on, Tej, you never come. What a night it is! We'll sing; we'll dance. Just play 'Purani Jeans' once. Please,' he said like a child.

'Okay, but no more than two pegs …' said Foxy.

'Oh, sure, sure, come, come. Ha ha ha ha ha ha … Lady in red is dancing...' Tanker sang in his hoarse voice, with a Haryanvi twang, spinning on his foot and draping his arm around an imaginary maiden. As we moved in the corridor, a frail *matka* stopped Bajrang in his way and told him to stop shouting. Matka is what we call the M.Techs studying in IIT-D. Bajrang clutched his collar and lifted him two feet in the air and roared, 'Who are you to tell me what to do!' and then swung him in the air, resuming his 'Lady in red is dancing …' and dropped him on the ground.

'See what I do now!' cried the matka from the ground.

Bajrang didn't even look back, and kicked open the door in his usual style. I don't blame the matka for what he did. I myself find these binges too painful on the ear and have done my share of complaining. I had watched the same matka grumble for the whole sem and shout his empty threats, but no one bothered about him. He was the sole M.Tech in this wing of the most notorious B.Techs and thus, had no say. We moved into the room where the aroma of hot pizzas had lost to the overwhelming reek of rum, whisky, vodka and what not.

We congratulated Chaapu, who was a teetotaller himself, and the topper of his Mechanical Engineering batch. There must have been ten or so packed in the room. Two or three were extremely drunk and the rest were on their way to glory. I took a customary sip or two of vodka.

I began with 'Purani Jeans', moved on to 'Papa Kahte Hain' and then to 'Summer of '69' and so on, the usual popular campus songs, while all around me clapped and some sang in their trembling voices; and so we moved on into the wee hours of the morning. By then, some had retired to their rooms after puking, some had retired without puking, but Bajrang was still alive, drinking as he usually does like a tanker and, surprisingly, was much more composed now. Meanwhile we chatted on with Chaapu who proudly gave us tips on how to crack job interviews. There were just four of us left in the room, when we heard a knock on the door. Bajrang shouted, 'Which sonovabitch is it?'

'Radhaswamy,' came the voice from the other side.

'Which Swami?' asked Tanker. It was the unmistakable South Indian accent of the matka. I never knew he was called Radhaswamy. We all knew him as matka only.

'It is that matka again, Tanker,' informed Foxy.

'The bastard wouldn't listen. What does he want, now, when no one is making noise? It seems that the lesson was not enough for him!' Tanker took a bottle of soda, opened it with his teeth, shook it hard and then pressed his huge thumb against the hole, while the gas hissed out.

'Open the door, Tej,' he told me. I did as directed, eagerly waiting to enjoy the fate that awaited the poor creature. The door opened and Bajrang sprayed around the contents of the bottle in wild frenzy. I stood laughing as I saw Radhaswamy drenched in soda with horror on his face. But I had to stop soon as I noticed that, for some reason, Chaapu and Foxy had frozen in between. Bajrang continued and Chaapu rushed to stop him. I peeped out of the corner of the door which blocked my full view and I shudder to write about what about I saw.

✒

To be honest, nothing comes to my mind, when I rack my brain to think of a thing that might have produced the same kind of horror even in a life so full of mishaps. Never until this moment had I known anything to boomerang in this fashion, and this a prank, where my role was not more than that of the hopeless extra who dances behind the hero.

Without testing your patience any further, I'll tell you that I saw three portly gentlemen as wet as three towels, behind Radhaswamy, who I didn't take more than a nanosecond, if that's the smallest second, to recognise and sport the same petrified look as that of my friends. Sir Tanker had washed two of the most important gentlemen in IIT, and third, the most important for me, not with water but with soda and thank god, soda, not champagne.

There they were, as menacing as the three musketeers: Prof P. K. Dhingra, Hon. Dean of Undergraduate Students; Prof. Keval

Chadda, Hon. Warden, Karakoram House, my hostel that is; and Prof. P. P. Sidhu, Hon. Head, Industrial Tour Committee. I couldn't believe his presence. You expect a warden and a dean to be on round to catch defaulters but not Prof. Pappi. I couldn't see any reason for his esteemed attendance there; except that god had finally decided to annihilate me and do so in the most destructive fashion. It would have taken a minute for a man of lesser intelligence, but for me it hardly took seconds to realise that there went my chance of skipping the industrial tour. I must say that a man of lesser mental strength would have jumped out of the window with it, but I stood my ground.

There was what one could call a killing silence, for what one could call an aeon, after the last spoken words of wise Chaapu, who had wasted no time in whispering loudly in the ears of Tanker (who had lost his sense of distinction in the extreme state of inebriety), that it was none other than the dean on whom he had been lavishing the froth. It was broken by none other than Tanker and in such a frightful fashion that I wonder, still, what I had done so grossly wrong in this life or the previous one to land myself in that hell.

I'd like to reproduce the exact conversation or monologue, to be precise, that ensued:

Tanker: Oh, hullo, old man! What brings you here? (silence, spectators look on, incredulous)

Tanker: Why, of course, what a fool I am to have asked you that question! You are here for the party, aren't you? Chaapu has bagged a top job, prof, and you, no doubt, want to congratulate this precious stone. Come in! Come in! You two also! Everyone is welcome! This Chaapu is a generous soul. (silence)

Tanker: And who are these cute little old men with you? (Goes up to the Warden, looks down at him with keen interest and points a finger) I have seen you somewhere, haven't I? I fail to place you, but you are most welcome too, what should I mix for you? Oh, I know, TEJ (he shouted), vodka and Sprite him!

(I swear I heard that ol' harmonica play again. Only the tune this time was sinister. Why on earth he should have called me to do the honours, I fail to see, but blame it on my bad luck. Or Mr Fate, whose presence I had begun to associate with the harmonica. There were two more students in the room and I was no expert barman, one of those who juggle with bottles and pour a drink from a mile above without sprinkling a drop, but still he called me, and I felt like one of the arms, right or left, whichever is stronger, of an underworld don, who is about to get the same sentence as his boss. Presently the Tour Head gave me an obnoxious stare as Tanker moved towards him. A card hung down from his neck and I knew, like Holmes, that the inscription on the card held the clue to whatever he did in this room. I couldn't read more than SALAD, written in bold, capital letters with something small beneath. What could salad mean? Presently Tanker, in his third attempt, grabbed the card and tried to read.)

Tanker: You still wear I-cards, old man? Funny! (roars with laughter) You don't need it; you are not a kindergarten kiddy.

That was the final straw. What had so far been a monologue was interrupted by Pappi. You don't expect professors, drenched in soda, to like being addressed as kindergarten kiddies, and neither did Pappi. He roared, 'You bloody fool; do you not know what you are saying and where it'll land you? You will not be spared. As the head of 'Society Against Liquor And Drugs', I assure you and your friends that I will not rest till I have you out of this college.' This was the not-so-jovial side of the otherwise jovial Pappi that none of us had witnessed before. We were given summons to our court martial the following morning. The 'Dis. (ciplinary) Co. (mmittee)' was to decide our fate, which indeed looked bleak.

❧

Though everyone will tell you that Disco is not the best thing that can happen to you at IIT, no matter how groovy it might sound, I wasn't very worried about its decision. A man in the throes of this queer thing called love doesn't worry about trifles such as suspensions.

How I would get away from Pappi was a question I didn't want to think about. He had my application with him. It hadn't been signed and wouldn't be signed. I could scarcely believe my misfortune. How on earth could they convene a ridiculous body called SALAD and make the Industrial Tour Head its president! How on earth could I be caught for an offence of drinking when I had just wetted my lips! And how in hell could Bajrang turn into a professor-annihilating Tanker! I couldn't sleep the whole night thinking about the absurdity of it all. Once or twice, I thought of calling Shreya but did not. To worry a girl at three in the night with such shockers is not the conduct of a gallant man.

⁂

In my introduction of Tanker, I forgot to include a thing or two, which Who's Who(s) will not dare to omit in the years to come. I hasten to correct the error for it is vital to the story. Tanker or Bajrang, as Who's Who(s) should list him, is the absolute king of *jugaad* – India's own word for resourcefulness. Tanker has all the links in the world and seldom does he leave a seeking soul sorry. He is the undisputed king of politics, that form a vital part of one's stay at IIT, and has devoted his life to it, and it seems that he would stay on here forever if there was not a clause in the IIT rule-book that states '... a student must not take more than six years to complete his degree ...' It was Tanker's sixth year and the authorities were already fretting, faced with the task of dislodging the monster from his den. Reminds me of a story about Hanumanji, after whom Bajrang is named, in which he blocks the path of mighty Bhima, who only unsuccessfully tries to lift the monkey-god's tail.

I felt we'd escape, and that 'we' strictly excluded Tanker; but I was proved wrong, and rightly so. I committed the folly of forgetting Tanker's talents. The gist of the story, without increasing its length or suspense, is that Tanker got away and saved us unscathed too. How he produced medical proof that his wild act was nothing but an epileptic seizure is an amusing story, but must be excluded here. No real case could be formed against us, and, in the comedy of errors that followed, we were warned that we were on probation for the rest of our stay at IIT.

The recent developments – the Disco meeting and the sleepless night had left me weary. And I slept like a log once I got back. I remember my crazy dream, in which the invading Pakistan army had come as far as my house, and the entire mantle fell upon my heroic shoulders to save the colony. I was surprised to see that Pappi and the dean were fighting for the Pakistan army, when I suddenly heard a bang ... and again ... and again. I feared that my house would be destroyed in that shelling when another bang woke me up. Relief, which came to me on discovering that my room was safe, was momentary, as I noticed that an idiot was banging on my door and calling out my name. It was Dusky. He had made a habit of waking me up. Whenever I slept, he came quickly, like a nightmare.

'What do you want at this unearthly hour?' I asked.

'It is noon, my friend, 12'o clock to be precise.'

'Oh!'

'And get ready, Pappi has called you.'

'Me?'

'And he is livid!'

'Oh!'

'Did you submit the interim project report?'

'No, when is the deadline?'

'Morning class at nine for which you didn't appear. He was very cross at that. The whole junta submitted.' He would eat me for lunch for sure. The fact that I had thought he was a gem just a day ago brought no solace.

'How could I attend his class when he himself caused me to land in front of the Disciplinary Committee?' I asked frustrated.

'Point. Are you sure you and Foxy got away?'

'Later. Don't frust. Let me get ready!'

Reflecting on my chances to meet Shreya, I moved on to his highness's room and he ushered me in after my polite, 'Sir?'

He arose from the pile of books and looked at me like a dad eyeing the lover of his daughter.

'Mr Tejas Narula,' he started. It is not often that I am addressed as 'mister' and when I am, it generally spells doom, 'I did not get your interim report.'

'Sir, I was at the Disciplinary Committee inquiry.'

'Inquiry indeed, we'll come to that later. How far have you reached in devising your cylinder?' he thundered.

'Sir, I am working on it ...' I did not know what to say for I hadn't even started, but fortunately or unfortunately, he didn't let me speak and interrupted, 'I'll tell you how far you have gone. You have gone as far as a deadbeat can go after bunking all the practical classes.'

'Sir?' I wanted to say that I had not bunked all the classes but wasn't given a chance.

'I know how to deal with rogues like you!' Gone was the nasal twang in his tone.

'Sir?'

'Don't go on mumbling sir-sir, you think you are very smart? You will get away with anything? You were the one, if I remember correctly who sought permission for not going on the industrial tour. Right?'

I wished I could have said 'Wrong' but I was helpless. I just nodded in approval and tried to gulp in the shocker. I knew he would not exempt me from the industrial tour and that meant death.

'What did you say you had to attend? The marriage of your brother? Let me check that with your parents. You think you can bunk anything?'

'Sir ...' Hell ... I had not thought of that.

There was in front of me a different Pappi, a Pappi who was about to spoil his record of not failing a student ever, not the Pappi whom I had labelled a gem, not Pappi at all but Prof. P. P. Sidhu. The previous night's insults had been too much for him. I agreed, but felt unlucky to be singled out. Why hadn't I worked on my project?

'I told you to shut up! What do you boys think of yourselves? It is a shame to have students like you at IIT. You are a disgrace! Utter disgrace! You were laughing while your friend was showering whisky on three professors. On three gurus! You know who a guru is? We used to touch our gurus' feet everyday! Every single day, you buffoon and that is why we are blessed with such life and knowledge.'

'Sorry sir, but ...' I wish I could have told him that it was soda, not whisky, and that I had goodness in me.

'Sorry! Sorry for what? The British left but left their legacy, sorry! Damned word ... You think because I am friendly with students you can take any liberty? You fool! I have been such an understanding professor all these years, ask your seniors, and this is the way you treat me ...' he was hurt and all his anger was coming out, 'And do you feel sorry? Not a bit! If you were sorry, you would have apologised in front of the committee today but what do you do? You cook up a ridiculous tale of your friend being epileptic! I couldn't believe it when the committee told me. Epileptic! My foot! Never have I heard of such sacrilege! You think it was all a joke? You might have been given a reprieve by the committee, but there are other ways to punish, and better ones. Put that in your head, that I am not going to let you off. I will not rest till I have set you right! I have it from my sources that you are a good friend of Bajrang and you were a part of this derisive conspiracy.'

'Sir, I did not know about it!' I said, defending myself. And I was honest. The number of charges he had levelled against me was amazing. 'Honestly, sir, I was unaware!' I said, almost pleading.

'Honest! That will be confirmed soon. I know you are a liar, I have seen your conduct this semester … you attend classes as if you're doing a favour to me! Yet, I give you one chance; I am going to call your father and check if your brother is indeed getting married. If this is a lie, then god save you! Wait here, while I call the undergraduate office to get your phone number!'

He picked up the receiver of the phone and dialled the internal number for the UG section, the office where all the student records are kept. I felt like what a victim must here felt when his head was stuck in a guillotine in those beastly times. The ground escaped from under my feet. My knees grew weaker as I waited for the call to be picked. I gave up. I could do nothing but stand and stare at my fate being altered right in front of my eyes. He'd tell dad how gloriously I had insulted my gurus by spilling whisky on them. It was the end. But what hurt most of all was that I would not be able to make it to Chennai. I started to wonder if I'd be able to meet Shreya ever … that her dad was against me and would never allow her to come to Delhi.

I closed my eyes as Pappi spoke, 'Hello UG section, Prof. P. P. Sidhu here. Good morning, can I have the number of a student …

Yes ... Tejas Narula?...Yes, home telephone number ... He is not there? When will he be back? Okay, yes ... Okay, yes,' It was good to see his 'okays' back, 'Call me after lunch then ... yes, after two, fine ... I'll be in my room after one ... thank you!' I opened my eyes.

He had put back the receiver and looked at me. That ol' harmonica was back on again. I finally drew my breath. I had got a lifeline and I was not going to lose it. I thanked god silently while Pappi told me, 'So two it will be then! The man who looks after the records is out and will be back then. He'll call me and give me the number. I don't want your number from you. Get out.' I said sorry again and rushed off. There was no time to waste. It was twelve thirty, according to the professor's clock. I had ninety minutes to save my life.

Ninety Minutes

I woke Foxy, who was resting his drained, though considerably less than mine, nerves with some sound sleep. Then I told him and Dusky about my near-death experience and that I had eighty minutes to prevent the catastrophe.

'We will have to prevent Pappi from taking the call.'

'But how, boss?' Foxy asked.

'By keeping him out of his room when the call comes.'

'But, won't the UG section guy call again?'

'No, he won't, because I will take the call as Pappi.'

'What?' Dusky asked, puzzled. I told him and Foxy the plan. There were risks, yes, but they had to be taken. It was a role tailor-made for Foxy. We waited for Dusky's reaction. Even if he was apprehensive, he did not show it.

He merely took a deep breath and asked, 'What's my role?'

Foxy reached the UG office at 1.55 p.m. and with innate coolness, asked for the official who kept the students' records. He hopped to him and informed him that Prof. Sidhu had sent him to get the required phone number. 'Tejas Narula, isn't it?' the official asked and started searching on his old computer.

At that moment, Foxy gave me a missed call and, having got my signal, I reached Pappi's room and saw him lost as usual in a heap of books. I stopped at his door and started wailing for pardon. As expected, Pappi told me that it'd be of no use.

Meanwhile, the UG official had completed his search and as he started scribbling the number on a piece of torn paper, Foxy gave a missed call to Dusky. Having got his signal, Dusky dialled Pappi's mobile. Foxy sat down in front of the official. He had to keep him engaged for some safe seconds. He began a cheery conversation with the official as he handed him the number.

I waited there, each second killing me, nervously anticipating Dusky's call on Pappi's cell, and then it came. Pappi was startled at the sound of the ring, as if woken from a deep slumber. He looked at the cell phone like he had looked at Bajrang the previous night.

'Mobiles! They have eradicated all the peace from this world … worse than nuclear weapons and yet one can't live without them.' He kept staring at the mobile and a nervous thought crept into my head … what if the fool didn't take the call! I prayed anxiously. But just at the moment his 'Jingle Bells' ringtone was about to die, he picked up the phone.

'Hullo,' he said, 'Hullo, who is calling? … I see … yes … hullo … you can't hear me? … hullo … yes, I am on the bio-bus project …'

Meanwhile, at the other end of the line, Dusky played around coolly in a business-like manner. He had called from a new number the moment he got Foxy's missed call, and was playing his part to perfection.

'Yes sir, I can't hear you at all; I am Prashant Oberoi. I wanted to speak to you about the funding of the bus …' said Dusky.

'Funding, oh yes …' replied Pappi ecstatically.

'Sir, I think you can hear me but I can't at all, could you move out?' asked Dusky, according to the plan.

'Hullo … okay, let me move out … hullo … is it clear now … no? … hullo …' and with that Pappi moved farther away from the room into the open ground in front of his room. He didn't even look at me in his excitement, as I had envisaged.

Biobull had saved me and it was the beginning of a beautiful friendship.

I gave Foxy a missed call. That completed the missed call network. And so Foxy got his signal too. He had the paper with my home phone number in his hand and was biding the time by entertaining the UG official with some cricket talk. Right when he got my call, he got up abruptly and told the official that he had to go somewhere urgently; so couldn't give the message personally to Prof. Sidhu.

'Could you please call Prof. Sidhu and give him the number now? I have to meet another professor in a minute. I got his call just now. I don't have time to visit Prof. Sidhu.'

The official, who had been humoured adequately by Foxy so far, obliged and picked up the receiver to call Pappi's office through the internal telephone network. With Pappi safely outside, I ran in, quickly picked up the call after half a ring, nimbler than any panther would dream to be.

'Professor Sidhu?' said the UG guy.

'Yes,' I said in a low, nasal tone.

'Sir, your boy had come to me and asked for the number.'

'Yes, yes, give me!'

'Sir, it is 0129 – 2284804 in the name of Dr Narula.'

'Okay, thank you,' I rushed. 'Sir, anything else?'

'No, that will be it, thanks,' and with that I quickly replaced the receiver and dashed out of his room to join Dusky. I just about managed a glance at the professor. He had his back towards me and was still talking, with his right hand gesticulating as if cutting a watermelon.

I reached the Ex. Hall in a flash; Foxy was already there. I couldn't believe my eyes when I saw that Dusky was still talking to Pappi about Biobull.

'Control your enthu!' Foxy said to him.

Afraid that he might overdo it, I signalled him to get over with it quickly. 'Welcome to the gang, maggu. We'll have more cons for you in the future. For now hang up.'

He did it by telling the professor that he had in his mind big plans for Biobull. As soon as he cut the call, he shouted 'Cracked it!'

'Did you intercept the call?' he asked and I gave him a high five and whooped, 'Fundoolicious!'

'What was that?'

'Oh, it's a word we use in ... nothing!'

'Your turn to speak to Sir Sidhu, now, Mr Foxy! Enjoy!' said Dusky, laughing.

'I hope you are clear ...' I added cautiously.

'Chill, man!' he said and with that picked up the receiver of the internal phone that lies in the Ex. Hall.

'Professor Sidhu?' said Foxy, 'Sir, you had asked for the number ... yes sir ... sir, there is no landline number in record but his father's mobile number ... will that be fine, sir? ... very well, sir ... 9899399772 ... Sir, anything else?'

'No, that will be it, thanks,' replied Pappi. Foxy had given my mobile number to Pappi. I'd have to change my number but that was fine. Thus it was finally my chance to talk to the great man.

In a second I got a call from Pappi which was short and sweet.

'Hullo, is that Dr Narula?' I said I was and asked who he was. He said he was P. P. Sidhu, professor, IIT Delhi.

'Good afternoon, doctor. I just wanted to speak to you about your son!'

'Hope he hasn't done anything wrong, professor!'

'No, no, no, no! I just wanted to inquire about your son's marriage.'

'What! He is barely twenty one.'

'Oh! Not him, doctor. Tejas told me his brother was getting married!'

'Oh! Why, of course, he is! On 14th Dec, engagement on 12th. Oh you scared me, professor!'

'That is it, doctor, I just wanted to confirm, there are so many boys claiming their brothers and sisters are getting married to bunk this industrial tour that I had to check.'

'You did the right thing, professor. I hope Tejas will get the permission, professor. Vineet is returning to India after two years … just to get married, and Tejas must spend time with his brother, I hope you understand.'

'Yes, yes, I do. I will grant him permission.'

'Oh, thank you, sir, I am obliged, thank you!' The 'doctor' hung up and so did the professor, both satisfied; and thinking alike that the world wasn't that bad a place, after all, contrary to what they were thinking a few moments ago.

⁊

And so, finally, I got my much needed sleep, which was interrupted, not before I had a livening chunk of it, not by Dusky this time, but by her call. She was naturally surprised to hear my sleepy voice at eight in the evening.

'At this hour, Tej?'

'Oh, I have been sleeping for the past five hours, Shreya.'

'Are you alright?'

'Now, yes!'

'What do you mean, "now yes"'?

'That is a long story.'

'And you are going to tell me.'

'But of course!'

'Hope everything is alright!'

'Now, yes!'

'Stop saying "now yes" and tell me what happened!'

'Tell me Shreya, have you read the Sherlock Holmes story, *The Boscombe Valley Mystery*?'

'You know I haven't read Holmes!'

'And how many times have I told you to read him?'

'Will you tell me what happened?'

'Not until you read Holmes.'

'Shut up and tell me. Have you gone mad?'

'Considering the number of risks I am taking to meet you, yes, I have gone mad. Very much so! The road to Madras, I tell you, is full of landmines, but let it be known that it doesn't bother me the least!'

'Why do you say all that?'

'Okay, okay I will tell you ... but the reason why I alluded to this "Boscombe Valley Mystery" is that ... if you had read it, you would have understood my position better, with my situation being similar to that of the innocent young McCarthy, except that he was charged with a much graver crime, that of murder ...'

'Tej, are you going to tell me?' she roared, and that pleased me. There's nothing better than getting the better of girls, who usually get the better of you.

'Wait a sec, darling. Sherlock Holmes quotes in this very story that "Circumstantial evidence is a very tricky thing, it may seem to point very straight to one thing, but if you shift your point of view a little, you find it pointing in an equally uncompromising manner to something entirely different".'

'Eeeee,' she uttered, 'I am hanging up, bye!' Girls say bye at anything and everything.

'Okay, now I'll be serious, senõrita. I merely quoted Holmes to ask you to etch in your mind those golden words before you brace yourself to listen to this most interesting narrative, as Holmes himself calls his cases ...'

And I told her all about the lavish bestowing of soda, the three M, the invention of the seizure, the Pappi outrage, the guillotine, the near-death experience, the miracle, and the extremely well-crafted, ingenious and what-not plot that saved the day; and I did so, as methodically and meticulously as I have told you; employing all the liberty that a narrator has in his hands, or say mouth, to add as much spice as he can to extract as many 'what', 'oh god', 'eeee', and 'don't-tell-me' from a chicken-hearted lady listener.

'Tej,' she said at the end of it, 'Are you sure you want to come?'

'How many times do I have to answer that question?' I asked tenderly.

'Till I am sure it is absolutely safe!'

'Which it'll never be! One cannot stop crossing roads thinking that the next truck will smash him to pulp ... are you crying?'

'No!'

'Yes, you are!' I said coolly.

'No, I am not!'

'Don't lie, as if I am deaf! Look at the way you are talking, like a small baby.'

'So what?'

'Why?'

'What why?'

'Why are you crying?'

'Just like that!'

'Ha ha ha ha, just like that!' I said imitating her tone.

'Don't copy me!'

'Is there a copyright?'

'Yes there is! But you can. Special privilege,' she said like a child.

'Oh, thank you, ma'am, I am honoured indeed!'

'You should be,' she continued in her three-year old tone.

'Now tell me, why were you crying?'

'Offo! Just like that, I was thinking … that you are taking so many risks to meet me … just me!'

'So?'

'What so?'

'Do you want me to meet more girls once I'm there?'

'Shut up!'

'What's there to cry about?'

'There is!'

'I can't see!'

'Because you are an idiot, dumbo!'

'That you remind me regularly enough, but tell me, why were you crying?'

'Offo! I got sentimental thinking about how much you love me …'

'By the way, I am not doing all this only for you. Get that notion out of your head. I am doing this for myself for I cannot go on living without seeing you for so long. And to think that your dad won't allow you within a light year of me according to his whims, drives me to despair. Thus I have to do something!'

'But … please make sure there are no problems at your home or college!'

'Oh, no problems, ma'am! You are saying all this when the lord (read Prof. Sidhu) has himself descended to earth and given the go-ahead … not to me, but to my dad, no problems now! The going is as smooth as a baby's bottom!'

'As smooth as what?'

'Baby's bottom, baby!'

'Where do you get such phrases from?'

'Oh! This, unfortunately, is not one of my inventions; I read it in a waxing salon ad, get skin as smooth as a baby's ...'

'Oh my god!' And she giggled finally.

'Good to see the rose back on your cheek, and now keep it right there; laugh and celebrate, for I am coming and coming with a song on my lips and a bag on my hips!'

'Hips?'

'Oh, I had to rhyme it with lips. This one's my invention. Nice?'

'Dreadful!'

'Fundoolicious, I think. Hey, you know what?' I asked, suddenly getting an idea.

'What?'

'I have decided to write a book, a book about my voyage and what all I had to do to meet you. It is so exciting.'

'It'll be a best-seller for sure!'

'I was thinking ... if I should bring my guitar along!'

'Not a bad idea if it is not cumbersome!'

'A little yes, but, wouldn't it be lovely to play it on the beach, jamming with the waves?'

'It will be! I'll love it!'

'Remember the last time I played it for you?'

'As if I can forget!'

'You looked like a goddess!'

'And you were "not bad"!'

'The terrace!'

'The beautiful night!'

'Your exquisite black dress!'

'Your "not so bad" white shirt!'

'The smell of wet sand!'

'Candles!'

'Dancing with you!'

'And your song!'

'Magical night, surely!'

And we went on talking about that night.

Monsoons; this year

Monsoons had arrived on time, betraying the unpredictability one associates with them. They have this habit of embarrassing the meteorologists, year after year, by rubbishing unabashedly all forecasts, from the time of their arrival to the time of their departure, and everything that happens in between.

Never is a season more welcome. The first drops washing away the fire of the earth. Never are the colours of the trees and mud so brilliant! Never is the breeze so intoxicating! Never is the poet so inspired!

I welcomed the monsoons as I always do, but this time not just for the rejuvenating showers, the picturesque boat in the puddle, the wet fragrance and the joyous, riotous football match in the rain. The monsoons this time had brought with them much more.

Shreya had arrived in Delhi with the monsoons on the 28th of June as if they had had a secret pact. And the romantic weather had a never-before effect on me. You could see Tej with a subtle smile on his lips, only when he was not singing songs; playfulness in his heart and a spring in his step. Life had never been better. I composed about a dozen songs and was playing the guitar all the time I was not with her.

But what those divine monsoons must be remembered for is a single evening. It was a magical evening. She had long wished to have a candlelight dinner with me. But girls, in this otherwise democratic part of the world, are not allowed out after the sun has set. It was, therefore, with considerable astonishment, that she exclaimed when I suggested we have one: 'Are you serious!?!'

I said I was and she asked me if I was drunk, to which I replied that I was not.

'Then how come you are getting such insane ideas?'

'Not insane, romantic!'

'But impractical! Tej, do you think I'll get the permission to stay out after six or seven in the evening?'

'No!' I replied coolly.

'Then?'

'What then? You don't need any permission! When did I say you need it?'

'Of course, I need it. Now, don't suggest that I should sneak out of my window at night ...'

'No, ma'am!'

'I hope you have not planned for the candle light dinner with a little assistance from sun. What's the idea?'

'When is your friend's sister's wedding?'

'Fourth of July.'

'And you have got the permission to attend it. Right?'

'Yes!'

'Then we don't need any other permission.'

I booked a place near college for dinner, rather I should say that Bajrang booked it for me. We had once had a party on its terrace and I had been smitten by the ambience. The terrace was usually reserved for parties and called for a hefty sum, but the owner was Tanker's pal. I don't know how and don't wish to know how he found out that there was no party on the 4th and had the entire terrace booked for me at no extra charge. I couldn't believe it when he told me, but, then, Tanker has his own impeccable style. 'No fight, brother. Both of you must be alone; why should morons interrupt you. I would hate that myself,' he had said to me and I felt extremely pleased to have a pal like him.

Her friends smuggled her out from the wedding and dropped her at eight as promised.

'We'll be there at nine thirty sharp, jeeju,' said one and then added teasingly, 'So be done with all by then. She'll also need to change back to her lehenga and that takes time.'

I thanked them, promised them a treat, bade them goodbye and looked at Shreya, who, all this while, had been concealed by the giggling girls. She smiled, knowing that I had been knocked out by her spell and whispered, 'Where shall we proceed?' and I mumbled, 'Upstairs.' I kept looking at her and she crossed her arms, pursed her lips, raised her eyebrows and shook her head at my behaviour.

'Come on, now, Tej, I am not looking that good.' But she was and she knew it.

She wore a black dress that ended just above her knees and settled gracefully on her curves. The black of the dress matched with the colour of the night and contrasted beautifully with her fair arms and neck, which glistened in the moon light. She wore her usual make up, that consisted of a line of kajal and a touch of gloss on her lips. She didn't need any more. Her silk-like tresses were open as usual, thrown back, shining silver at places. And she wore the silver earrings that I had gifted her just the day before. For the first time with me, she wore heels and that brought her almost to my height – thankfully, not above it.

I took her burning hand in mine and led her up the stairs, and she was surprised to see the setting. She pressed my hand, looked into my eyes and said that it was gorgeous. It was an idyllic terrace – no roof on the top, just the sky studded with diamonds.

It had rained in the evening but the rain had stopped, the heavy clouds gone, to display a spectacular star-studded sky. Thin foam-like clouds still spattered here and there added to the beauty. Though the clouds had made way for the stars, the smell of wet earth lingered on, wafted by a brilliant, cool breeze – the hallmark of monsoons. The moon was out too and bathed the night with its silver splendour.

Out in the left corner, near the fence, were two wooden chairs with a table in between. On the table, two long candles illuminated the setting, and the silverware cast their light and reflected the moon's. I had chosen that corner as it was the most exquisite one, overlooked by a Gulmohar tree with its ready-to-bloom orange flowers.

I pulled a chair for her and said, 'Ma'am, have a seat.' Lately, I had realised, she allowed me to look into her eyes. 'Hope the place is not bad, ma'am! All your humble hero could manage!'

'Not bad? Shut up, Tej!'

'I could not afford a five-star,' I said. Her family was much more well-off. Time and again, this gap bothered me. Leave treating her lavishly, I couldn't even afford balcony tickets for movies. The rates had soared to a hundred and a fifty each.

'How many times do I tell you not to talk about expensive dinners and gifts? You never understand. How many times have I told you, I am a normal girl, who likes simple things in life? I am an average girl who likes to eat her five rupees orange bar, who likes her junk jewellery over gold. Please Tej, understand ... that I am NORMAL. N-O-R-M-A-L,' she spelled it for me, 'let me enjoy these things, and stop worrying about treating me like a queen. I know how much you love me and that is it. I won't embarrass you by asking how much this place has cost you but I know you have sacrificed for it. Tell me, how many weeks have passed since you last saw a movie?'

'Leave that!'

'Now, why should we leave that? When I say leave all your nonsense about money, you don't!'

'Okay, sorry!'

'You already insist on paying the bills every time. Can't we go dutch, once?'

'No, I think we have talked about that enough too,' this time I roared. I was very clear on that. That was the least I could do for my princess, I thought. I belong to the school that believes in thorough chivalry. A ridiculous movement was sweeping the town and guys were doing all sorts of insane stuff like getting facials and manicures, and asking their girls to give their share of the check. The roles were shifting in this modern society and it sent in old hats like me, a shiver down the spine. Whatever happened to the toughness that separated a boy from a man and, more disturbingly, to the chivalry and courtesies that we had been taught, with which a woman ought to be treated. Anyway, I was completely an antique and had made it clear to Shreya, and in no uncertain terms, that, 'We might have to live like squirrels and nibble at five rupee sweet buns if I don't have adequate money, but no way, mind you, no way, will you poke your hand in your bally purse. Do you get me?' I had asked and she had got it. She didn't bother carrying her purse after that and thanked me for that. It was a lot of hassle, she said.

'Anyway, leave all that,' I resumed.

'Yes. Lovely sky, fresh air and you. What else do I want? To think of a five-star cluttered with old people who would rather die than raise their voice! One can't even breathe there!'

'Exactly. Better to be at a dhaba!'

'I swear!'

'Where one can breathe, yawn, sing or dance and pick one's nose!'

'Yuck, shut up!'

'And what a vulgar price to pay for a dish of dal that my mom cooks better!'

'Exactly!'

I called for Michael, the waiter, who was told to wait downstairs. Dinner arrived and it was heavenly to eat together as the two candles lent our corner a glow.

'What would you like to drink?' I asked

'Water!' she replied.

'Wine?'

'Shut up!'

'Michael!' I shouted.

'You shout for Michael as if he is your younger brother.'

'Oh he is, sort of,' I said, as he hurried up the steps and arrived with a skid. I asked him to fetch two glasses of orange juice from the juice shop below.

'You look beautiful, Shreya.'

'How many times will you tell me that?'

'Till you tell me how I look. You haven't even said one word in praise of this handsome young man!'

She eyed me from top to bottom of what was over the table and said, 'Stand up first!'

'Why?'

'I should get a full view.' I stood up. One has to agree with girls.

'Hmm,' she said sinking back into her chair.

'Not bad!'

'Not bad?'

'Yes!'

'Great, thanks!'

'What do you want to hear?' she played around.

'Nothing!' I said.

'Offo, don't make faces like girls. Okay, you would have looked handsome if you were tall. Say six feet.'

'Oh?' I said and added peevishly, 'If height is such a problem, get yourself a basketball player.'

'But I don't like tall guys; after all, I am just five feet three.'

'Two and a half at full stretch!'

'Whatever, so five feet six is perfect for me.'

'Six and a half inches!' I corrected her.

'Whatever,' she said.

'No whatever, you borrow half an inch from me and add that to your own height. Wow!'

'You look so cute when you are irritated!'

'Oh! Now I am cute. Not "not bad"?'

'You are cute and it is good you are not very tall. You look perfect, like my small baby. The white shirt looks nice. Happy?' she said so sweetly that one had to be happy. I had bought the white shirt at her request.

We finished our meal and I looked at my watch. It was quarter to nine. Forty five minutes had passed just like that. And the next forty five would fly the same way. I wished time would stop. I moved my chair next to Shreya and told her to listen to the rustle of the leaves of the Gulmohar tree as the breeze sifted through them. I took her delicate hand in mine and looked into her eyes, and we both enjoyed the silence as she gently placed her head on my shoulder and nestled close. I could feel her breath on my neck. I wanted to kiss her on her lips but had promised her I would not, until she asked me to. I observed her features in the moon light. I kissed her forehead and then her soft hair, and she kept still. Her fresh hair was between my lips, and I was lost in their fragrance. Those were blissful moments.

I gently removed from my pocket the earrings that I had brought for her today. One pair of earrings a day she had demanded. I showed them to her as they glinted in the moon. 'Are they pretty?' I asked.

'Yes!' she said.

'Now get up, time for some surprises.'

'Can't we just sit like this for some more time?' she asked in a subdued voice.

'I wish we could for the rest of our lives, Shreya!' I said and called for Michael. She lifted her head from my shoulder slowly and got up. 'Do you remember the deal we made when we first met?'

'That guitar and dance one?'

'Yes, time to act.'

'But where is the guitar?'

'Here it comes,' and Michael entered with a black guitar that I had borrowed from a friend. 'Here's a song I composed … after that you teach me how to dance.'

'Okay,' she said surprised.

'Michael, you may go downstairs now.'

Instead of proceeding, he produced from his pocket a shining silver harmonica.

'With your permission, sir,' he said and before putting the instrument to his lips, winked at me.

'You surely don't know the tune, Michael,' I replied fearing the worst. Even if he had the knowledge, he replied with shrewdness which wouldn't have disappointed Mr Fate, 'I will try to catch up, sir.'

'But wait! This is surely not tuned with the guitar.'

'I took that liberty, sir.' He winked again.

I pretended not to have noticed. 'Then let us start,' I said, excited, as I slung the belt of the guitar over my shoulder and plucked a few strings. Michael put the harmonica to his lips and Shreya was left bewildered.

'Ladies and gentleman, wherever you are hiding but listening,' I started, 'Here's a song written especially for this girl sitting right there, yes, that one who is giggling. Let me introduce my band. Michael on the harmonica and Tej on the guitar and vocals. The drummer was drunk, and being a little short on funds, couldn't arrange mikes; I hope that is okay.'

Shreya said 'yes' and I began plucking the strings of my guitar softly, and listened to the rhythm as Michael started playing his harmonica. It was perfect, and after the intro I began to sing as the chords changed from D to G to A to D again. It was my Dylan phase and thus the song had to begin with an 'ain't no':

I ain't no rich kid, just a poor nerd,
I've got no money, my pocket's full of mud.
Faded jeans and ragged shirts, thank god, they are in,
For those are the only things, I have to fit in.
If you're the kind of girl, who just goes for money.
You can check out Michael (she laughed),
He's got a big limousine.

All I have got is unconditional love.
All I can promise you is I'll be there when the things are tough.

No lousy music, my guitar gently plays
A song, written, especially for you, babe.

All I have got is unconditional love.
All I can promise you is I'll be there when the sea is rough.

The soft plucking of the guitar notes blended with the rich sound of the harmonica, and my serenade was a success. We both bowed after the performance, while Shreya looked on overawed. Michael knew it was time to leave and I told him to put on music.

Then Shreya got up from her chair and gently kissed me on my cheek. She whispered she loved me. I really wanted to kiss her then.

'So, you want to learn guitar?'

'No, not today, but I will teach you how to dance,' she said.

'Hmm, not a bad idea considering we have just twenty five minutes left.'

I had prepared a playlist of some soft instrumentals, mostly in a four by four beat, which I thought would be appropriate for light dance. Presently the music began to resonate creating a magical aura. The first tune was 'Ave Maria' by Johann Sebastian Bach, one of my favourites, and one on which I had always dreamt of dancing with a girl.

Shreya closed her eyes, listened to the beat, and then looked at me. 'It is lovely,' she said, 'Now, you don't have to do anything, just follow my feet. When I go right, you go right, when I go left, you go left. We'll start with these basic steps. Okay?'

'Yes,' I said, lost in her eyes and perfume. She took my hands and placed them on her waist, then she placed her hands on my shoulders and we kept looking into each other's eyes. She moved gracefully, three steps to the right, and then three steps to the left, and I followed hopelessly, not caring about my feet, but just her eyes. She kept up patiently with my clumsy movements. It took me quite a while to get those six steps right, after a lot of tripping, falling and balancing, but once I got them it was a joy to move with her.

It was effortless, and we both had drowned in one another's eyes. She came closer and closer, it seemed, and I smouldered in the warmth of her body. Time and again, I'd caress her hair; time and again, we'd talk in soft whispers and our breaths got lost in each other's. Time and again, my hands brushed against her arms; time and again, I thought I would have no sadness if I were to die thus, in her arms.

She taught me how to spin her, and that was the best part. It was a treat to watch her spin so elegantly, as her hair brushed against my face again and again, and immersed me in its perfume.

Soon we resumed the six basic steps she had taught me. It was heavenly.

'Let's continue this only,' she whispered.

'Michael,' I shouted, 'Play track one and repeat it till the end,' and with that 'Ave Maria' was on again.

'Can I kiss you?' I whispered.

She merely swayed her head to signal a no. I was not disappointed. 'We are dancing, Tej, maintain the sanctity of the art,' she whispered back.

'Hardly five minutes left, your friends must be about to reach.'

'Yes,' and with that she drew me closer and we were lost in the embrace. It felt then, I distinctly remember, like our souls were one.

November, that year

I was fast asleep, curled up like a dog, on the concrete bench installed outside my classroom. One assumes it was installed by a magnanimous soul, to provide rest and air to tired students in between lectures.

It was November already; the temperature was falling like a child who has tripped off his balcony. And the sun-bathed bench was just the thing one needed. It was seven forty-five in the morning to be precise. The class started at eight and I had no business to be there fifteen minutes before, nor did I intend to, yet there I was, as unmistakable as the remarkable sun of that very morn. The credit for the achievement must go to my sister Sneha, and so should the blame for my half-dead state. She kept me awake till four in the morning, talking about Shreya.

She was aware of the developments that had taken place between her brother and her best friend since that movie incident. She was startled when she came to know about it but, like all shocks, it had subsided. She was supposed to drop me at my college but unfortunately, it turned out that her class that day began half an hour early at eight. As a result, I was dropped off like a sack of rotten potatoes at IIT Delhi at seven-forty. I couldn't have been sorer with her, with her denying me sleep and then slapping me in the morning at seven, telling me sharply to brush my teeth. Such is life with sisters!

Somebody patted me hard on my back. I opened my eyes with great effort and saw the haze clear gradually. Even if the haze had persisted it would not have been too difficult to deduce who that colossal figure was. It was Dusky who, as you know, had made it a hobby of his to wake me up. His eyes were wide in disbelief; he pinched his cheek and then uttered a howl. It had hurt. It was all for real.

'Has the sun risen from the west or what?'

'Are you frust with life or what?' I asked, annoyed that I had to be woken up to answer such a dumb question.

'Have you seen the time? Still ten minutes to go.'

'That's the very thing I should say to you. Ten minutes to go, you maggu, and you wake me up! Every time I sleep, you are there to do the honours!'

'I wanted to check if it was really you here with ten minutes to go!'

'I was here when there were twenty minutes to go!'

'So you have finally decided to listen to my advice, and are mending your ways. It'll pay you, friend, and pay you well. You will see your C.G. (grades) soar.'

'I have not decided on any such stupid thing. It is a mere accident that I am here and I hope life doesn't play such a trick on me again.'

'God only help you!'

'I tell you, Dusky, just once, only once, I ask of you, cast all your fears aside and lie cosily curled up in your blanket and savour the joy that comes from it. Then, only then, will you relate to my funda. You will see this world with new eyes, my friend. You'll be a changed man! And trust me, it'll all be for the better,' I lectured my friend who had a habit of arriving for class at such unearthly hours, and that too after a bath, as if they were giving gold medals for the first arrival. The clash of our philosophies went on for a few minutes when, suddenly, I remembered. I had to ask him a question that had slipped my mind in that state of half-sleep.

'So have you shortlisted the prof?'

'Which one?'

'The one who'll be with us on the industrial tour!'

'Didn't Foxy tell you?'

'No.'

'I didn't decide, yaar. Pappi called me himself and said that he would go with us on the tour.' That hit me. As if a sock had been soaked with water, whirled in the air and hurled straight at me. Those were ominous beginnings. I wondered if it had anything to do with me. I remembered his words: 'Put that in your head, that I am not going to let you off. I will not rest till I have set you right!' What could he be up to? He had granted me permission to miss the industrial tour. What could he gain by accompanying us on the tour?

'What happened? Why are you stunned? You have got your permission. So you needn't worry!' said Dusky.

'When did he tell you?' I inquired.

'Friday only!' It was almost eight by then and my classmates had started coming in. Presently a circle of bewildered souls surrounded me; some slapping, some pinching, some pulling at their hair in order to make sure that it was not a dream. Was it Tejas Narula there, for real? At eight?

The class which was spent by me in analysing Pappi's action came to an end, and the next two hours were free. I wearily got up and followed my friends out. Dusky stopped outside the Mechanical Engineering Department office. 'Wait a second, have to meet Sandhu for my project,' he said. Meanwhile I leaned against the wall and talked to Foxy. We both had not dared to take up any extra projects. Compulsory courses were already too much of a burden.

I heard Dusky shout for me. It sounded out of place. 'Maybe sadist Sandhu is strangling our friend's neck,' remarked Foxy. But we met him well and good outside the professor's room before the department notice board. 'Look,' he said, staring grimly at the board.

'You know we don't bother about deadline notices …'

'But it doesn't deal with that,' he said with a chill in his voice that made me uneasy. I went closer to the notice board, half expecting to see words written in blood. It was nothing of that sort. It was a simple printout on a plain letter-sized paper.

DEPARTMENT OF MECHANICAL ENGINEERING

NOTICE – By the order of Dean, UG

1. All students are hereby informed that they must produce documented proofs if they wish exemption from the industrial tour. In case of a marriage ceremony, the wedding card must be produced, and likewise for other reasons.
2. The documents must first be submitted to the Tour Guide, Professor P.P. Sidhu, who, after his approval, will forward the application to the Dean, UG, for his validation.
3. The leave will be granted only for the days of ceremonies and one day extra for travelling purposes after which the student must report to the tour. Under no circumstance will the student be allowed to miss the whole tour. The tour is a part of the curriculum and thus a prerequisite for the B. Tech. degree.

Prof. P. P. Sidhu – Tour Committee Head and Tour Guide
Prof. P. K. Dhingra – Dean, Under Graduate Students

I withdrew from the cluster that had formed around the green notice board. The notice was not there for the Mechanical Department. It was there for me. I knew others would be granted permission in the end. But I was not depressed.

❧

The only thing that I said to myself in the following days was, 'Think, Tej, think!' I had a particularly favourite teacher in high school, Mrs Bhatia, a delightful lady who had this favourite line ready, whenever we failed to answer her questions, 'Put on your thinking caps, children!' Whether I found my thinking cap or not, I would certainly have made Bhatia ma'am proud, for I did arrive at a solution. I decided against mentioning all this to Shreya or else she'd tell me not to come again. But, having come so far, I was not going to retreat.

Tanker lit a cigarette and sank back into his chair. Smoke rings appeared out of his nose and mouth. He flicked off ash and looked at me, disappointed. Then he spoke: 'You have let me down, brother … after all that I have done for you!'

Elder brother was unhappy that he had been kept in the dark and was not a part of the planning commission. But today, I had to tell him, as I needed his help. I honestly considered him a good friend but hadn't told him because there was every chance that he might blabber something out while on drinks.

'You really love her, brother!' he said, smiling.

'Leave all that, yaar,' I said, as I avoided such remarks as a rule.

'But you do … taking so many risks … I must say, listening to your tale, I want to love someone too,' he said and Foxy and I were surprised. The tough Bajrang was talking about love. 'So … what do you want me to do, brother?' he said, tapping at his cigarette again.

I told him the plan. I needed a wedding card, reading 'Vineet weds Preeti' or any other lady, 14th December, which excused me till the 16th, after which I needed to hop off to the Inter-IIT sports meet. There was nothing else that could save me. And, for that, it was required that I be part of some team. But then, teams are not as readily available as lottery tickets, and that too at the crunch; unless, of course, you have Tanker as your guardian angel.

'It is imperative that I go to Inter-IIT post-marriage. Any team for me?' I asked Bajrang.

'Shot-put,' he said coolly and there was a funny silence. Then Foxy started laughing, clutching his tummy and looking at me, the subject of the joke. I weighed a mere sixty kilos.

'Shot-put?' I asked, unbelieving, 'The game in which you have to throw a ball weighing a ton as far as possible?'

'Yes,' he said coolly again.

'Do you realise that the ball is heavier than me?' I asked wisely.

'Don't you worry about the technical details!'

'Do you realise that the profs won't allow you to take a handicapped person with you?' I tried to reason.

'Don't you worry about the profs!'

'I don't believe they will allow him for shot-put,' interjected Foxy.

'I don't say things just like that, you buffoons. When I say he is in the team, I mean he is in the team. No one can throw the put better than me. I can go alone and they will not complain. They know that all the medals will be ours. But rules say a five-member junta must be sent, and so be it. Thus even if I take along four paralysed maggus, it wouldn't make a difference. Don't you worry, no fight, brother.'

Foxy and I looked at him, amazed. A man of resources, if ever there was one. A gem of a friend. Other people would have laughed at me, if ever they saw me in the shot-put quarters, and mistaken me for the chap who draws the chalk-lines. But here was a man who saw potential in me, a mere duckling. Once, in my school days, I had tried my hand at it, this whole business of shot-putting, and had putted the shot with full force, and expected it to land out of the school, but my expectations were short lived: the put landed right on my foot. Never in my life did I try juggling with puts again. The pleasant thought was that, of course, I won't have to do it this time. It was all just a cover up.

'So happy, now?' inquired Bajrang, 'You attend the marriage and then hop off straight to the sports meet. And the tour is killed, nothing of it remains. Zook,' and at that he chuckled.

'There is still a problem,' I said, 'I haven't yet told you about the main part of plan.'

'What is it now,' both my friends asked in unison. For them the battle had been won, the enemy trampled and the flag unfurled. But I knew better. It was alright, this whole combo plan of wedding and sports, brimming with *masala*, but it still left my enemy with plenty of room. It foiled the enemy's current strategy, but didn't eliminate the enemy, and I knew until that was done, the battle was not won.

'Pappi has to be removed,' I said and a deafening silence ensued. Both my friends looked at each other and then at me, stupefied, with bulging eyes, as if a dragonfly had landed on my shoulder which must be squashed, but with caution. I looked over my shoulder, first right and then left. There was nothing save my blue shirt.

'Come on. Not that big a fight, brother, to start removing professors,' Tanker replied shocked.

'But he has to be removed.'

'He has kids, goddamit!' cried Foxy.

'Where do the kids come in now?' I asked innocently.

'You idiot, who'll take care of them?' And then I followed their train of thought. In the grim aura that had been created, they had started to think like the mafia. One couldn't blame them.

'I meant, removed from the position of Tour Guide,' I replied.

'Oh,' said Tanker and Foxy.

'How will you do that?' asked both.

'He'll be forced not to come.'

'How?'

'I'll make him an offer he cannot refuse.'

'What offer?'

'Biobull!' I stated and laughed sinisterly. They both looked at me and joined in too. The laughs dissolved in grim silence. I picked up my guitar and started playing the immortal tune of the Godfather. The professors had dared to displease the Godfather, I told myself, and they must not be spared.

Still November, that year

I leaned against the barriers at the airport and craned my neck to see if he was there. All I saw were three charming girls; part of the airline crew.

Don't imagine too much, I warn you all, if you've begun to suspect my attendance at an airport. To disappoint you eager beavers, whose minds have been corrupted by an overdose of thrillers, I merely waited for Vineet, my brother, who, I promised you all, has no small role in these memoirs. He is a real chum. There are some jobs that even sisters can't do which underlines the significance of brothers.

I was there to receive him at the airport in absolute secrecy. It was supposed to be a surprise for the whole family, his arrival, and only I was let in on the secret, partly because we two are really close, but mainly because somebody needed to arrange a taxi.

Presently I saw his head appear, his body hidden behind two pretty girls. I was sure he was following them. Some people never change. Then I saw his neck emerge, then the belly and I could see him wholly now, shoving his trolley as the two girls turned left. I could see a hint of disappointment in his face. He had grown a little fat.

'You saw those two girls?' he asked me, his eyes opened wide. No hi, no hello!

'Yes,' I said.

'Stunners they were, bloody, turned left!' he said frustrated, 'Anyway, wassup, brother? How's Shreya?' I was greeted with a real bear hug.

'Good.'

'All well?' he asked.

'We'll talk about that in the taxi,' I said as I took his trolley and directed it towards the stand. With the luggage shoved in the boot, and both of us settled snugly, I ventured to explain to him the situation.

'My dearest, respected, elder brother,' I began, as is my wont, whenever I want anything from him, and he interrupted, as is his wont, understanding that his younger brother required his services. And past experiences had taught him to keep a mile from me, when I was in such a mood.

'I have just landed, brother!' he said, giving me one of his looks of suspicion.

'I'd be the first to wish you rest, brother, but I am afraid, this thing needs to be done quickly or I'll be doomed,' I said to explain to him the gravity of the situation.

'You'll never change, will you? I was so happy … living a life of ease and peace … continents away from you … and a minute with you …' my brother said dreamily.

'Don't begin, brother. It is just a tiny task and you are just the man for it. What a deuce of a situation I would be in, had you not come!'

'I hope I had not!' he said.

'Now listen, don't make a mountain out of a molehill. It is child's play, this task; yet, it needs a man, and none to beat you.'

'Which man?' he asked suspiciously.

'Oh, I'll come to that.'

'Tell me all,' he finally said, yielding. He knew, of course, that I was going to meet Shreya, but nothing beyond that. Nothing about my tête-à-tête with eminent professors, and all the planning thereafter. I narrated it all with the required stresses, and saw the effect I wished to see.

'Damned unlucky of you to land in such a soup,' he said commiseratively.

'Don't call it a petty soup, brother, it is an ocean full of alligators,' I corrected him.

'I have to admit that it is not your fault this time and my heart goes out for you!'

'You have a heart of gold, brother. Twenty-four carat if there is no carat above it. Help me; you are the only one who can!' I looked at him with melancholic eyes and he melted.

'Alright, what is it?'

'We have to remove the professor.'

'Well thought. How do you go about it?'

'I don't go about it, big brother; it is you who will go about it!'

'Oh!'

'Yes!'

'How?' he asked, nervous like a man about to jump in an ocean of alligators to save a drowning friend.

'The professor is hell bent on going to the tour and there's just one thing that can prevent him.'

'What?' he asked with an air of a man about to be told the darkest of secrets, not sure if his heart would be able to cope with it.

'Biobull,' I said with the air of a man telling a secret.

'Biobull?' he asked, not knowing what to do with it. And I hastened to clear the haze. Biobull – the pride of the professor, the bus that will rock the world. Biobull – the bus that runs on gas made from human waste. Biobull – the professor's dream. Biobull – the thing that the professor will do anything for! I gave my brother all the definitions that the lexicons would supply in centuries to come.

'Biobull!' he said with a sigh, as if it was his lover's name.

'Yes, Biobull,' I asserted again, 'Biobull, the future of locomotion!'

'Biobull,' he repeated, not able to get over the repulsive word, 'What a frightful name!'

'I know, but that's what it is, Biobull, and we needn't worry about it. All we should worry about is … what all can be done with Biobull!'

'What all?' asked my brother, innocently.

'You should ask what cannot be done with Biobull. We can have an alternate fuel, we can save humanity, counter global warming; we may never have to worry about saving power. Imagine serving the world by sitting on the potty. You'd be a millionaire, brother, with your current excreting abilities,' he eyed me; but I resumed, 'What can't Biobull do, brother! It can bring about a revolution and, more importantly, for us, brother, it can prevent Pappi from embarking on the tour!'

'How?' he asked again, piqued to the extreme after listening to such drivel.

'Ah,' I said, 'Your focus impresses me, never the one to stray, here's how! You just need to go to him, and tell him that you are an NRI entrepreneur, who is interested in putting all his life's savings, which incidentally run into millions, into this gold mine of a project, the famous Biobull! And that you'd be coming to India again in December, the 13th of December to be precise, and will be here till the 20th; those are the industrial tour dates; and thus both of you can work together during that period. If he asks you to arrange a meeting some other time, give him a flat no. Convince him to meet you in December. This, for you, Mr CEO, will be an enriching experience, considering you intend to do such idiotic things for the rest of your life. Thus he will be prevented from going to Pune! He won't risk losing out on such support for his dream project! Isn't it a peach of an idea?'

I must say that I wished to see, in my dearest brother's eyes, a spark, a relief that the world, after all, wasn't a boring place, and still offered us, albeit occasionally, moments worth remembering. I aspired to see the zeal of his younger days, those wonderful days, when we went from place to place, shattering many a window pane and lamp shade. However, I was shattered to see his eyes. In place of a glint, there was gloom. His look was of a man who had finally decided that it wasn't wise to jump into the ocean. Touched he was to see his friend drown, but could not risk alligators.

'Sorry, brother,' he said plaintively, 'I cannot do that.'

'Why?' I asked.

'I won't advise that, brother, I don't want you to get into any trouble. I tell you, these professors are merciless. They will ruin you if they find out.'

'How the hell will he find out? It is perfect, my friend, and you are the man for the job.'

'You always say so, brother!'

'And I am right, am I not?'

'Not always!'

'Always,' I asserted.

'Remember … when in class six your father was summoned by your moral science teacher to complain to him that you had hit her with a piece of chalk?'

'I had not hit her with chalk. She had hit the chalk instead. I had merely thrown it in the air, it was a bloody coincidence that she appeared out of nowhere and collided with the missile. That was most unfortunate. She lost an eye for a whole week.'

I corrected him again.

'Whatever, but chacha was summoned, and you did the same thing then, that you intend to do now!'

'Come on, not that brother!'

'Why not? It is exactly the same. You made me appear before that brute of a lady as your dad and it was all a dud. She saw through it all in three seconds …'

'She had to see through it all, brother! How on earth could she believe you're my father? You are hardly four years elder to me, and, I remember, your front two teeth were missing then. It was an error, brother, and I admit it! Ingenious though the plan was, of replacing my dad, it was also immature. It had a fundamental flaw. I chose the wrong man for the job. But then I had no option, brother. Now, I am in third year of college and there is maturity in my plans! You should be proud of me, and look at you, you shudder like a rabbit! Whatever happened to the spirit of the Narulas?' I asked, appealing to his self pride.

'My only concern, brother, is that it shouldn't harm your career in any way.'

'It will not, don't you see the ingenuity of the plan?'

'I see the risk too; we shouldn't do it!'

'Fine, let your brother drown,' I said.

'It is not that, brother.'

'It is much more than that. I see my brother of yonder years, one whose eyes shone at the hint of mischief, is dead,' I began my emotional blackmail.

'Not the case,' he waved it off.

'The very case. You are a coward now with no sense of adventure.'

'That won't work, brother.'

'Please, brother, please,' I pleaded, 'Just once … remember our days of glory. When we walked arm in arm, shattering windows, flowerpots ... whatever came in our way. Just once ... let us relive them brother ... You come here only once a year! And I miss all our adventures. I miss the time we spent together. I miss you, man,' I bellowed. I could see his eyes get dreamy and misty. After all, how could he forget those times? 'Remember those golden days, brother. The teasing girls, the shoplifting, the thrashing I once got for puncturing Mr Dhanpat's car tyre, the way we used to run away after ringing doorbells, and the five-star where we demolished that ... what's his name ...'

'Gobardhan!' my brother replied eagerly, clearly transported to the era gone by.

'Remember that lizard you flung on that rat of a girl? How can you forget all that? Where's that spirit?'

He came closer to me and put his arm around me. 'I miss those days too, damn it, I miss those days. And here, your plan is just the one for a soul like me. Reminds me of our favourite Fatty of Enid Blyton, the one who used to disguise, impersonate and what not ...'

'And you are fat!'

He gave me one of his looks and then laughed. 'And I am fat. I wanna do it, bro, but are you sure it's safe? I'd love to help you and Shreya. But it should be safe ...'

'Have you lost your famous vision, brother? You should have analysed the situation yourself and declared it as safe as a Swiss bank locker. You let me down. You want me to explain it all to you. Spoon-feeding, that's the phrase. I see all these years out of India have taken a toll on you, and all that astuteness of yours has eroded. But this plan will reactivate it all, brother. It'll be an elixir for you.'

'Fine, I'll do it; after all, the professor doesn't know I am related to you ...'

'You are the man for the job. You fit to a tee the image one needs. It is like this role was written for you, brother. You still don't look like my father, but you look like a young corporate investor, one of those who make millions before they are thirty!' I saw him dream again, 'I can see you wrapped impeccably in a tuxedo, and boy, don't you mean business!'

'Make that a black tux!' he added.

'Fundoolicious!'

'What was that?'

'That's a word we use in college. Perfect, the man in the black tux, stepping out of his black Jaguar, with his black briefcase, going to the professor and telling him, 'I want to invest a few millions in your bus.' Isn't it chic?'

'I wish he was building a jet.'

'One cannot have it all, brother, bus it is, for now,' I added with empathy.

'When do I meet my client?' he asked.

'Tomorrow, after we discuss at night what all you need to tell him. You are the man, brother. And the best thing is that you have done your studies in entrepreneurship. You know all that crap about venture capital, angel capital ...'

'Don't worry about all that, brother, it'll be done.'

'I knew you would do it. Thanks.'

'Mention not,' he said, and with that I slipped in his hand his new visiting card. 'Prashant Oberoi' – it announced in impeccable black over a smooth white – 'Venture Capitalist, Make Millions Bake Billions Inc., Austin, Texas.' A man in a black tux, in a black Jaguar, with a black briefcase, was definitely not complete without those. My brother looked at it, felt it and flashed a smile of 'Well done!'

✍

I waited for him at the Holistic Food Centre along with Foxy and Dusky. He had taken a long time. What if he couldn't pull it off! It was a winner, the idea, yet the way Mr Fate had taken a disliking to me lately, anything could happen. He called; I nervously pressed the button to receive his call, praying silently that all was well.

'Hullo, what happened?' said my voice, shaking.

'Come out of the campus to the coffee shop, now!'

'What are you doing there?'

'Will you come?'

'But tell me what happened or my heart will fail.'

'It's a long story.'

'Alright, will be there in five minutes.'

He was acting like a brute. Prolonging the agony and making me miss classes. All along the way I prayed for his victory over Pappi. I could see his colossal figure through the glass. He was dressed in a formal shirt and trousers. He sipped cold coffee and eyed a girl as usual. We entered, took our chairs, and I hoped the greetings would be short and sweet. But my brother has no sense of timing. There I was, under such enormous strain, and he talked about girls. It is all very well to talk about girls, a pleasure always, but there are times one wishes to talk business.

'Isn't she hot?' he said, rolling his eyes in the direction of a pretty lass.

'Will you tell me what happened?' I asked, trying to be cool.

'She has been looking at me for so long,' he chuckled.

'She has to look for so long; it does take an hour or two to look at you fully, from the right end to the left! You fat rascal. Creating unnecessary suspense. Calling us all the way here! Will you tell me what happened?' I said, this time bringing my fist upon the table. Heads turned and so did the head of the girl who was 'eyeing' my brother. She was pretty.

'You call me rascal? I am not delaying, you knucklehead! I called you here because it was not safe to meet inside the campus; your Prof. Pappi walked with me to that food centre where you wanted to meet me. It would've been hell had he seen us! You are a complete jackass!'

'Tell me what happened. I can't take any more, brother!'

'He isn't going on the industrial tour ...'

'You did it, brother?'

'No, you don't understand, he wasn't, anyhow, going on the tour ...'

'What?'

'You are saved ...'

'How do you know?'

'Because he refused outright to meet me in December, and I saw our plan failing ...'

'Then? Didn't you entice him with the two million dollars investment?'

'Didn't work.'

'A production capacity of hundred buses a day?'

'Didn't work.'

'Selling the technology to the US and EU?'

'Didn't work.'

'That it would be India's biggest achievement since the discovery of zero?'

'A zero effect.'

'That scientists from Germany and Japan were working on the same lines and their patents must be beaten ...'

'Nothing worked.'

'What is he doing in December?'

'Turns out his partner's daughter is getting married in December. He got to know about the dates only now ...'

'His partner?'

'Yes, his partner on the Biobull project ...'

'That's great ...'

'Wait ...'

'What now?'

'You'll faint when I tell you where he is headed for ...'

'Where?' I asked quickly, before my mind could run amok.

'Chennai ...' he said, and I fainted. But I wasn't allowed to enjoy my unconsciousness. My mobile howled. I clumsily took it out of my jeans pocket. It was Bajrang's call.

'Hullo, Tej?'

'Yes, brother!'

'Bad news, yaar!'

'What?'

'The wedding card can't be printed!'

'Why?'

'It is damn expensive.'

'How much?'

'Minimum two thousand rupees!'

'I just want one, yaar, I heard it costs about fifteen a card!'

'Yes, but the template of the card costs two thousand! They don't care if you want one card or a million; they take separate money for the template formation!'

'Okay!' I said dejected.

'No fight, brother. We'll find a way, and then you are on the team. Keep the enthu high!'

'Yes, thanks, bye!'

'Bye!'

Brace yourself for life, I often say, for nothing is more unpredictable. However, I couldn't help but droop like a withered flower after the twin shocks. News of the wedding card was, no doubt, unfortunate, but one didn't know what to do with Pappi's information.

'What happened?' was the natural question that came from all corners. And I told them. Obviously, I couldn't churn out a princely sum of two thousand rupees for one card. Already, I just about managed to make both ends meet with my allowance, and then, there was the forthcoming trip itself, where money would be needed for lodging and food, and regaling her highness. My brother, as I had foreseen, put his arm around me and said, 'I'll give you two thousand bucks, don't worry.'

'Shut up!'

'If that smoothens out things, why not? After all, it is hardly fifty dollars!' he said after his brief calculation. I told him to shut up once again. Money wasn't the solution.

'Boss, listen,' Foxy said, 'Now, Pappi personally gave permission to your father that you may skip the industrial tour. He doesn't think that you are bluffing, so I don't think a wedding card is necessary. After that you go to Inter-IIT, which is within rules. I think you can take a chance by skipping the industrial tour without any formal, written permission.'

Dusky concurred. My brother played with his hair. I thought. 'But there might be a fight, and then if by chance, my family is contacted by these professors, I'll be dead. You see, I can't always intercept calls,' I said.

'As far as everything is done within the rules, there is no problem,' summarised my brother, 'Given their dislike for you, there is a chance that professors cause a problem if you don't show the card and decide to skip the entire tour. They must be mad after being drenched in soda. What an insult! You shouldn't take any more liberties with these professors. Think of something within the rules,' he added wisely.

'And this industrial tour is a degree requirement. If they decide to go to the extremes, Pappi and the Dean, they may invalidate your tour, thus extending your degree,' commented Dusky. That hit me hard. An ugly scene conjured up in my mind. I was wishing my friends, clad smartly in orange graduation robes, with a wry sombre smile. There was Foxy, smiling and saying, 'Don't worry, boss. You'll get it too someday!' And Dusky saying, with his head swaying, 'I told you to mend your ways.'

People talked among each other, 'Disgraceful! Spoilt his parents' life for a girl!'

I drank two glasses of water, and then became aware of the conversation going on. 'Why don't you go on the tour and leave for the Inter-IIT sports meet on 15th, and then be with Shreya?' Dusky asked.

'How many times have I told you, I want at least ten days there! See, she is a girl and may not be able to get out every day, and if that happens, I would hardly be able to meet her. I am not going to reduce the length of the trip! No way! There must be a way!' I said.

'There is,' said Foxy, who was staring at the ceiling blankly.

'What?' I asked.

'Attend the tour with us!'

'How is that a way? I told you I am not wasting any days!'

'You won't!'

'How the hell?'

'Break your leg!'

'Break my leg?'

'Yes, break it. Reach Pune with us, and break it! Then obviously you won't be in a position to accompany us on our industrial visits … The doctor would have strongly advised fifteen days strict bed rest! If you get up, you may risk losing your leg forever. Thus you must rest and not move around,' he said.

'Genius!' I remarked, 'And the best part is that Pappi will not be with us. I wish he was not even in Chennai, but I don't think there's any chance of us bumping into each other. Now, Dusky will have to choose the professor who goes with us, and we'll decide together. We'll choose the kindest of professors who would not sense anything fishy and allow me my sweet and deserving rest. And then I'll sneak off to Chennai!'

. 'But how will you go to Chennai with a broken leg, you fool?' asked Dusky.

I could only smile at that. I saw that Foxy was smiling too; so was my brother, and, slow that he might be, my friend is certainly not dim, and, eventually, he smiled too, and remarked before any other could.

'Of course, you do not need to break your leg!'

The winter sun shone outside, and my life was trouble free once again. I could see Shreya, clearer than ever, waiting for me by the sea side. My hands automatically started playing bongo on the table, and a harmonica tune resonated in the air – Louis Armstrong's 'What a wonderful world!' I sang along.

I see skies of blue, clouds of white,
Bright blessed day, dark sacred nights,
And I think to myself, what a wonderful world!

November end–December, that year

The days were getting colder and colder as we moved closer towards what promised to be a chilly December. Jumpers and jackets were out, and it had gotten just cold enough to allow me the pleasure of breathing out white frost in the morning. The final semester exams were perilously close and most of the students had got down to serious studying. The Major Tests, as they are called, were to commence from the 3rd of December and go on till the 8th. I had calculated that I could not afford to give less than five days for preparation. It was the last week of November, already, and the date when I was to resume my romance with studies was quickly approaching. I had to work for long hours on my project too, that enigmatic cylinder and Professor P. P. Sidhu was keeping a close eye on its development. The professor had calmed down a bit after watching me sweat (if one can in winters) in the workshop. The cylinder was shaping out almost satisfactorily. It was official now that the reverend professor was not accompanying the students on the tour. My friends were also busy putting finishing touches to their projects and poring over their books. And well, I was busier than ever in putting finishing touches to my plan and dealing with the cylinder. Life was travelling at a breathtaking pace. Few days were left and there was much to do still. That the plan was changed at such a late stage did not help either. The last minute exigencies manifested themselves much like a flood. A new professor had to be chosen, a plan had to be made to 'break' my foot, and I still hadn't arranged for my accommodation in Chennai!

ᴥ

'This is the man I want!' I burst out on seeing his photo on the computer, 'He is the one!' His face was the most amiable one. He smiled out of his photograph harmlessly, and gave the impression of a man who'd have nothing to do with canes and cudgels.

Dusky showed Foxy and me the photos and profiles of the professors on the college website for selection of the Tour Guide. I had told him to research and find the coolest of all the professors.

He added this caption to our man's photo: 'He joined only a year back and thus is yet to learn the IIT custom. Reliable sources say that once, when a boy hit him with a chalk on his nose, he didn't rebuke him, and instead delivered a discourse on non-violence.' Add to this his friendly face, and you have just the man you were looking for – one who would look tenderly at a boy with a broken foot, maybe shed a tear, pat him lovingly, and order him to rest for a month. Mr Uttam Trivedi was our man.

ᴥ

'Uttam Trivedi', announced the nameplate in black and gold, 'Asst. Professor'. I knocked on the door.

'Come in,' came the call and in went Dusky and I.

They say photographs lie. One look at this specimen was all you needed to dispel that notion. The picture had only understated the amiability of his face. The man, even with his moustache, was the most harmless I had ever seen.

'Yes?' he said cordially.

'Sir,' said Dusky, 'I am Rishabh, the Class Rep of the Industrial and Production Department ...' and, after telling him about the tour, he asked, 'I'd like to know if you could accompany us.' He was extremely courteous.

'Where do we go?' asked our man.

'Sir, Pune and Goa,' I replied, adding as much courtesy to my tone as I could.

'Okay,' he said, thinking.

'Sir,' I added, 'Goa will be an enjoyable holiday for your wife and kids too.'

'Yes, yes,' he said, 'It'll be a nice surprise for Kittu!'

'Yes, sir, ma'am will be delighted.'

'Oh, no, Kittu is my son, eight years old!'

'Kittu, of course, will be delighted too, sir!'

I almost danced with joy in that moment. Things were finally falling into place. Dusky produced a sheet in front of the professor and asked him to sign.

'I love students,' he said, smiling one of his best ones, 'I never miss any chance of interacting with them.'

'Thank you, sir,' we both said.

'Just a minute,' he stopped us, as we were about to leave, 'What is your name?' he asked me.

'Sir, I am Tej. I am helping Rishabh with the arrangements for the tour. There is so much to do. I thought I'd lend a hand.'

'Oh, what a thought! Always help others.'

'Yes, sir, one strives to,' I replied and we moved out. I shook Dusky's hand. The work was done. Our man was in. Thankfully, appearances aren't always deceptive.

❧

You could say that I was on a roll. Things were finally falling neatly into their respective places. You are, I am sure, familiar with these events – if you have not been too bored with these memoirs of mine, and dozed off. The pages fluttered by a passing wind and waking you up, you assume that this is where you left off, for the page number tells you that the torture won't last for long – with the latest happenings, the withdrawal of Professor P.P. Sidhu and the quick appointment of a befitting proxy. And I am sure in the wake of these extremely desirable developments, you are saying to yourself, 'Ah! He has done it again; he is a man with the strongest willpower and the wickedest of brains! God bless him!' I take these compliments with a humble bow.

To find me hence with my head in my hands, a deep furrow in my brow and a brooding look in my eyes, you will, no doubt, be appalled. You will hasten, like a true friend, to tell me that the sun is out, and I should be swaying to salsa rather than sitting sadly on my sofa. But I will tell you the reason, and right away. It is damn difficult, I tell you, this bloody business of getting one's foot broken.

It seems simple, but when going a little deep into the whole matter, you would find it a muddle of the first degree. If you are not as dim, if I may use the reference again, as the bulb of my room, you would have gathered that I don't actually need to break my foot. I mean, I don't need to undergo an extreme test of valour, of sticking out my leg before a speeding truck, or smashing a mixer-grinder on my tender toe. I am lucky and I mean it. I have been spared that test. I saw a movie once, in which a dude was in much the same fix as I am now. The only way he could get away from some disaster, of considerably lesser scale than mine, was to break his foot. He was advised by one nincompoop to drop a typewriter on his foot. I was prevented from seeing the rest of the movie due to a power-cut but, now, my heart went out for him. He was not blessed with the company of my friends, or he would have been wisely counselled.

He would need to do exactly what I was going to, except that I did not yet know how.

Broken feet, for all their disadvantages – the pain, and that it is most inconvenient to romance a girl – have a distinct advantage. One doesn't need to find a doctor. I mean, of course, one needs a doctor to repair the damn thing but one doesn't need to find that doctor. Any doctor will do – anyone who knows his bit about the bones and the marrow. One need not organise a special search for a doctor. He could be any of the friendly neighbourhood faces we see with a stethoscope hanging around his neck. But the doctor one needs when one doesn't have a broken foot, and wants it to be proven broken still, is of a special kind. Our doctor may still be lurking in the neighbourhood but we can't be so sure as to be able to point to one and say he is our man! I hope my problem manifests its impressive magnitude before you. And I would be greatly impressed by those, who have, by the skilful use of that brilliant theorem of equivalence, replaced the problem of breaking a foot by the problem of finding a suitable doctor. Keep it up, you all; you need to put in a thought or two about making mathematics your career.

The problem that presented itself before me was a monumental one. I had to find a doctor, and of a special kind, who could lay his scruples aside and plaster an unbroken foot, and produce a brilliant medical certificate that strictly recommended bed rest. You could, of course, find such doctors; I knew some personally, but the sad thing was that they were all cooped up in this part of the country while I needed someone in that part of the country. Good old Tanker couldn't be of much help here. I wished I was a mafia don who had his left and right arms scattered all over the country and just a phone call would ensure that the work was done.

What rendered the dilemma even more complicated was the fact that I had just an evening for myself in Pune. We reached Pune at about five and I had about four hours to conjure up a doctor, a medical certificate, and then convince the professor that I was practically out of the tour. It could all go horribly wrong. The possibility that a doctor could eventually be found who would melt at my love story and help me was extremely rare. I might find a doctor, but the professor might not release me, he might want to watch over me caringly for at least a day as he was a gracious fellow. The problems seemed to be endless and hit me like a hurricane. But I was not daunted. I had to act and I realised that two things needed to be done quickly.

The first I did right away, for I could not afford to lose even a single moment. I took my hands off my head and used them judiciously to call my travel agent. I asked him to cancel my ticket and book one for the next day. One day less with my darling was better than not staying with her at all.

I got down to the second task in the next second. I had to find a doctor in Pune, not when I was in Pune, but now. I had one and a half days now, still, it was wiser to play it safe. It was an infinitely better feeling, I thought, to have a doctor or two tucked under my armpit than to search like a sniffer dog on the very last day. Hitherto, I had always been a man of the last moment but, now, I had to retire from my habit.

I was not a mafia don but I had my share of contacts. I listed the names of all my near and dear ones who were vaguely linked with Pune. The list stopped at five names. I called them one by one, hoping at least one would yield a doctor's name.

✐

As I stared at the list I saw the designs of Mr Fate again. I was plunged into the deepest of despairs. After two days of contacting the listed people, I had drawn a blank. Only one name remained on the list made according to priority.

Reading it only filled me with dread. I could not deal with her. I tried to steel myself and prepared to confront her. Midway though, I began to shiver and returned to my mobile phone. I could not deal with her alone, I concluded and dialled Shreya's number.

'There has been a minor change in the plan …' I began straightaway, business-like.

'What?' she asked perplexed.

I vomited everything fast – the change in the dates, the new scheme of finding a doctor, and the fruitless list. And then I just sat back and listened patiently to Miss Shreya's 'don't comes'.

'What can I do?' she finally asked.

'Call your friend.'

'Kamna?'

'No.'

'Does Saumya know someone in Pune?'

'Does she?' I asked hopefully.

'Which friend, Tej?' she asked nervously.

'We have got to tell her, Shreya.'

'No way,' she cried and hung up.

❧

She was in the room next to mine and I heard the 'What!' alright. I hoped that wouldn't wake up the parents. Then, like a veteran soldier I anticipated soft footsteps, and rolled in my blanket till it had wrapped me twice over. But my anticipation about the kick proved to be wrong, instead I was hauled out by the hair on my scalp.

❧

'It is no use telling me that there are bad aunts and good aunts. At the core, they are all alike. Sooner or later, out pops the cloven hoof,' surmised Bertie Wooster while speaking of his feelings for his aunts. You can replace the 'aunts' part by 'sisters' and that'd pretty much give you my outlook on sisters. I thanked god I had to face only two of them – one elder, one younger – though age hardly matters when it comes to sisters. A sister on her day is as bad as an aunt.

After hauling me out of my cosy winter bed, Sneha closed the door behind us and punched my midriff.

'Who all know?' she asked me.

'About what?' I acted and took a punch again.

'About your hideous plan.'

I remained tight lipped.

'Dusky and Foxy?' she asked and added, 'That can be excused. To save your life, give me no other name.'

On finding me silent she opened her mouth again,

'Ria didi?'

I nodded.

'Vineet?'

I nodded again.

'Am I the last one?'

'Papa doesn't know!'

'And you tell me only when you need me!' She delivered an upper-cut and shot out of the room.

✍

She wouldn't speak to me in person, nor did I have the appetite for more knock-out punches. It was all arranged as, what is known in this mobile age, a conference call through Shreya, though she herself didn't speak. And needless to say, we didn't need the whole arrangement. I could hear Sneha's booming voice from the next room, of course. Parents were not at home.

'What a lucky girl you are, Shreya and what a fool you are, Tej?'

'I agree with the first of your conclusions, but ...' I began.

'It is not worth it, Tej; I have given it thought. Too much risk is involved ...'

'I am going, sister!'

'Count me out then, I cannot help you!' What could Shreya do but remain quiet?

'Oh, don't say that, blood relation!'

'Blood? After all that you have done, mister, why should I?'

'Mister? I am your brother, elder to you if I may point out!'

There was silence.

'Fine, don't help me as a sister. But, for humanity, Sneha, for restoring faith in those virtues of benevolence and altruism that this world seems to have forgotten. Your act, Sneha, will make this world stand and introspect, and bow down in shame. The world will see you as a beacon of ...'

'Oh god! Where do you get all that crap from? Got a dictionary or something in your hand?'

'Oh no! Even if I had, I have not the skill of flipping the pages so quickly to find words that fit!'

'Okay listen, let's get to the point. I could help you,' she said, and I uttered a cry of joy, but right then she added, 'But ...'

'But?'

'But why don't you ask Ria didi?'

'Oh, Sneha, don't rub it in. I didn't tell you only because I thought you wouldn't permit me to go ...'

'And I do not ... but still for your faith ...'

'Help me!'

'Wait, did you ask Vineet?'

'Oh, Sneha! He's bankrupt when it comes to doctors …'

'And Tanker?'

'His network stretches as far south as Delhi …'

'Raju bhaiya is in Pune …'

'Who?'

'Shreya's brother who is getting married.'

'You want me to ask Shreya's brother? Are you playing around or have you gone bonkers?'

'Why don't you ask papa for the doctor?'

Father had graduated from AFMC, Pune and still had many friends there.

'You have lost it, sis. Thanks, it is a sound suggestion but he is not in.'

'I was not in until moments ago.'

That opened the old wound. There was silence again though I could hear a lioness breathing in the next room.

'Can you do the job at all or am I wasting my time?' I questioned her resourcefulness and that worked.

'Of course, I can. You need a doctor, right? Who'll plaster your leg and make certificates?'

For all of you perplexed readers, Sneha is definitely not in the league of Tankers when it comes to *jugaad*. She merely had a good friend studying medicine in Pune.

'The very man!' I exclaimed.

'It'll be done!'

'Are you sure?' I asked, stumped by her confidence.

'Yes, brother! It is a common thing!'

'You mean this breaking of feet? Is it so common in Pune? Slippery roads, I guess!'

'I mean false certificates, you fool. Students need them often for various reasons. My friend knows a couple of doctors who do such stuff!'

'Are you sure?'

'Don't bother; he is a real resourceful guy.' I conjured an image of Tanker in my mind. 'He said there was nothing to worry about, and it'll be done, and when he says …'

'"No fight, brother", there is no fight, sister!' I emphatically completed the sentence with Tanker's motto. 'You see, your brother is much the same type of guy, but his network ends in Delhi. He has been thinking of expanding his operations for long. I think your friend can be his aide-de-camp in Pune, what say?'

'I say you owe me a treat,' she replied to the point.

'Absolutely, sis! I'll have cakes and chocolates lined for you. I cannot express in words the gratitude I feel towards your esteemed …'

'Cut the crap!'

'Thank you!'

'That will be enough, bye!'

And I hopped into the room next to mine and kissed her.

That put a seal to the phase of planning. Just as I put the phone down, I felt a surge of relief, of work well done. I moved to the window in my room, and saw the sky full of stars. Life was indeed beautiful with her in my life.

Delhi Station. 10 December, that year

'Nizamuddin Station' said the blue board installed outside the station. Our car braked in front of it, amidst an ocean of humans. There were people here, people there; people, confusion everywhere. Some were loaded with luggage, some with children and others were just idling away, enjoying the ebullience of the station. Dad told us to get off, and said he'd join us at the platform after parking the car. I took my rucksack out of the boot and flung it over my shoulders, while Sneha handled my guitar and laughed at me.

'What is it?' I asked.

'Nothing, the bag is taller than you!' she giggled as girls do. At least all girls I know giggle.

'Shut up!' I said.

'Don't use such words,' said dadima politely, 'It is not auspicious.'

'From here,' guided my mom.

'I have eyes, mummy, I can see!' I retorted. My whole platoon had landed at the station to bid me adieu as foreseen. Only my dadaji was not there; his health didn't permit him. We passed the hall, where black screens depicted various train names and departure times in red. I looked up and saw that mine was leaving on time.

We climbed the stairs slowly, keeping pace with mom and dadima, and descended to reach platform number two. Trains and stations always fascinate me. It had been more than five years since I'd been on a train, and my heart brimmed with joy at the prospect of the journey. Nothing matches the colourful canvas of a station. And the romance of trains! Blue bogeys of my train shone majestically in the brilliant sun. On the blue part of the bogey, 'Goa Express' was written in yellow. The sight of the train, up close, after such a long time, filled me with childlike excitement. The carriage rested royally and seemingly went on and on into eternity. My fingers merrily touched its metal as I walked on.

The station was all chaos. Coolies, dressed in red, appeared out of nowhere to snatch your luggage. 'Why do you labour, sir? Give the bag to me!' I heard over the lady announcer's '… train will arrive shortly on platform number …' Tea sellers rattled spoons against glasses, and shouted in their shrill voices, the famous station slogan of 'Chai-Chai'. The vendors cried themselves hoarse to attract customers to their stalls, which served every Indian snack you could imagine. There were book-stalls, phone-booths, shops of knick-knacks. It was hardly a station, more of a bazaar, with all its hustle-bustle. There were people in all shapes and sizes from different backgrounds. Different languages were heard as I surged through the crowd. Nothing, I reflected, unites India the way the trains do. People from every part of the country are brought to the same bogey … from every stratum of the society to the same platform.

Never does chaos, the hallmark of our nation, look so picturesque. Never is it more colourful. Never does noise, a blend of the train's snort, the engine's whistle, the chai-walah's rattle, the traveller's murmur, bring such brightness to the heart. The sight of my friends took my spirit to an all time high. I saw Foxy, Dusky, Jasdeep, Manpreet, all chatting gleefully. Their voices hushed on seeing that I had brought my family along, lest their expletives be heard. There were other parents too, but no one had brought a battalion like me. Papa arrived and pleasantries were exchanged. The ambience was electric and the air was full of gaiety. A lot of bantering went on. My friends laughed madly, clapping excitedly; my mom smiled, so did my dad and Sneha. Dadima, not used to such fast paced humour, understood little, but flashed all her teeth. My mom decided to conduct an inquiry with my friends, 'How many shirts are you carrying?' Some said nine, some eight... Her eyes directed themselves at me, 'See, I told you,' and then she told my friends, how I insisted on taking only four shirts, and how she had managed to convince me to carry more.

Suddenly the professor appeared, with his wife and Kittu, smiling as ever, adding to the happiness. He wished all of us cordially and we responded in a chorus. He got busy with Dusky. Just about five minutes remained for the departure. People started climbing into the train.

I looked at my family. Sudden emotion hit me – 'How much I love them!' A foolish thought crept into my mind – 'What if something goes wrong ... and this is the last time I see them all?' I shoved it away taking god's name. 'Don't be foolish', I told myself.

'Goodbye,' I said to them, hesitantly. My eyes became moist. Not because I would miss them; it was hardly a ten-day trip. It was just that I was keeping them in the dark ... lying to those who had so much faith in me. I felt guilty. I wanted to tell them, 'I am not doing anything wrong, I really love Shreya ...' but would they understand? I wanted to meet Shreya, but didn't want to leave in this manner. I prayed to god again to set everything right, and told myself that I was just following my heart. I am not doing anything wrong, I repeated. Love could never be wrong.

I touched dadima's feet and she gave me her blessings. She thrust into my hands two white plastic boxes. 'Amla and chooran! Keep them. Your tummy is so sensitive! Eat carefully!' I nodded and smiled.

She had not changed at all since my birth. Her silver hair, simple sari, big glasses, her love and concern were a few constants in my life. I would know, only in time to come, their real value, the comfort that their presence brought to me. She took out some sugar from her little box and distributed some among all. It is a custom at our home. Eating something sweet before leaving is considered auspicious.

I hugged mummy and papa. Mom was sentimental as usual. 'I am not going to Kargil, mumma!' I told her.

'If only you were not so naughty, I would have sent you happily. Please don't get into any mischief,' she said, and I wondered if what I was about to do qualified as mischief. 'Walk carefully on roads, and don't play pranks on people,' and as I saw her eyes watering, I hugged her again. I tried not to speak for it would make me cry. 'And you haven't even brought a blanket, everyone else has,' she said worryingly.

'I'll share, mummy,' I managed to say. Dad was cool. He is never demonstrative. But he loves me no less. 'Enjoy yourself, son!' he told me, 'Have fun, but remember – everything in limits, and I know you'll bunk industrial visits, but do visit two-three industries, at least, and bunk carefully!' He knew me well. It was no use telling me to be diligent. He himself was the fun type. But he didn't know that I was going to bunk the entire tour.

My darling sister stood with her hands crossed and with tension all over her face. She had tried to stop me, but I had not relented. 'What if something goes wrong?' she had asked again and again, but I had waved off the question. 'Take care,' she said, 'Please be careful, bhai!' and pushed into my hand a folded piece of paper. I looked into her eyes and gave her a look of assurance. I kissed her on her forehead, grabbed my guitar and went into the train.

I took my seat and the train started to move slowly. There was so much noise in our bogey already. I went to the window and waved out to my battalion. I could hear mom shouting, 'Don't get off the train on the stations in between! Remember when you ...' A tear of guilt trickled down my cheek, and I quickly wiped it off.

My friends surrounded me. The fun had begun.

✿

I excused myself from the celebrations and quietly went to the end of the bogey. I opened the folded letter that Sneha had given me.

Bhai,

I couldn't say all this as mom and dad were there. Don't think that I don't want you to go to Chennai; it is just that I am extremely nervous. I will be till you return safely. Please be very careful! Don't take any risks. I know you live life king-size but once there in Chennai with Shreya, maintain a low profile. It is not only about you, but also about her well being. Meet her very discreetly; her dad shouldn't come to know.

Now remember to message me at least five times a day telling me what you are doing. Give my love to Shreya.

And yes, don't get off at the stations. Remember once when the train had started and you were idiotically buying magazines? How you managed to get on the train! Don't do that. Remember Mr SRK your Kajol is not at the station, she is in Chennai waiting for you. So stay on in the train.

And don't forget to bring me something from there.

Love, Take care.

Just then, Shreya called. I wiped my tears and drew a deep breath. 'Yes Miss Shreya, the train is on its way, I am on my way, Chennai beckons me and I'll be there soon, to hold you in my arms and ...'

I looked out of the open door. Vast open spaces rushed past. Trees, lamp posts, men, women glided away. I sensed how every second brought me closer to her.

❧

Often a problem with writing novels is that one has to follow a theme. Each incident in a novel must be linked to the central subject. One can't stray here and there too much, or else he'll be called directionless, incoherent and all those adjectives only critics have knowledge of. Therefore one has to painfully delete incidents, no matter how interesting, which though having occurred in progress to the climax, are essentially irrelevant to the theme, viz. the train incidents: 'When Dusky rubbed oil on an uncle's back', 'The journey of the stinking socks (of Jasdeep)', 'The Adventure of the Missing Blanket'. They have to be excluded presently. They can, of course, be produced separately as 'A Treasure Trove of Train Tales'.

However, at this point in the narrative, it will suffice to say that the train rattled and swayed all the way, and rattled and swayed to a halt at the Pune station at about five next evening. Thus I completed what can be called the first leg of my voyage. I was some thousand kilometres closer to my love and that brought to my heart a buoyant feeling. A small step it may be for others, it was a giant leap for me.

Pune. 11 December, that year

Doctor Prabhakar, our man, was not in. He was out on an emergency. It had been an hour since I left Ram Lodge, our residence, with Foxy and Dusky. Every minute added to the tension. I moved restlessly outside the clinic while my friends chatted on. Pinto, the person commissioned by Sneha's friend to help us, smoked nonchalantly.

'Man,' he said in a tapori *Mumbaiya* accent, 'You should smoke!'

'Should?' I asked, puzzled. He made it sound like a motherly advice.

'I should say you must!'

'Must?' I wondered if I had always been kept in the dark about all the vitamins and minerals that filled the cigarette stick.

'Yes, must! Look at you, man, moving about like a chicken. This,' he said, pointing towards his cigarette, '... cures it all. You feel low, you feel aglow, you feel crappy, you feel happy, howsoever you feel, this is your best friend; loyalest, I should say, if there is such a word.'

'There is no such word and, besides, what about the damage ...' I was about to begin a didactic discourse on the damages of the damn thing when a handsome man in his late forties, dressed neatly in blue, rushed past me into the clinic. He had a stethoscope around his neck and thus had to be the missing doctor. I must say that the sight of the physician didn't do anything to alleviate the tension that crushed me. The fact that he was so well dressed and looked like a proper doctor didn't go down well with me at all. I had expected the man to have a nasty scar or two or, at least, a big black mole somewhere on the chin. But he had none of the features that a man, if he churns out false certificates, ought to have. And that made me quiver.

I hadn't the time to look at his shoes and that bothered me. If only I had looked at his shoes. Shoes give away scruples, I have heard, and presently I prayed for dirt on the doctor's boots.

'Did you see his shoes?' I asked.

'Why the hell, man? Why should I look at his shoes?'

'Did you or did you not?'

'No, man,' he said, and resumed blowing smoke rings.

'No, boss,' said Foxy and Dusky on my questioning glances, thinking I was out of my mind. I pursed my lips. The mystery remained a mystery.

With each passing second, I grew more and more jittery.

'Are you sure he will do the job?' I asked Pinto.

'Man, you need a smoke!'

'Are you sure?'

'Man, how many times do I tell you?'

'He doesn't look like the kind who would do unethical work. You didn't even see his shoes.'

'What about the shoes, man? Screw the shoes. And, man, I tell you, he is a damn good person to do unethical work.'

'Then?'

'Then, what, man, he is a friend. I told him you had a severe family crisis and ...'

'Family crisis?' I shot out loudly with a look as if I had been punched in my belly.

'Yeah, family crisis,' he said coolly as if my family didn't matter to him.

'What family crisis?' I demanded, indignant that I had been kept unaware of any crisis, real or fake, which concerned my family. What if the idiot had drivelled on about death or a similar morbid event?

'I just told him, it is one of those things that you wouldn't like to talk about and he understood,' and at that I cooled down.

'Great, man,' I told him borrowing his 'man'. He was an intelligent guy. A neat excuse – a thing that cannot be talked about!

'So even if he asks, which I am sure he is understanding enough not to, just tell him you are not comfortable discussing it. Fine, man?'

'Yes,' I said and Pinto was called in by the doctor. He emerged in about a minute and winked at me. He patted my back and told me to go in. 'It'll be done,' he said.

I entered a little nervously. There was a look of condolence on the doctor's face. His eyes told me that they sympathised with my grief. He told me to sit and asked me,

'Are you fine, son?'

'Yes,' I said hesitantly.

'You should be brave, son, the night will pass,' he said. He thought of me as one of those unlucky sons of misfortune.

'Yes, doctor, I am trying my best,' I continued in my mournful tone.

'Listen, now; you want a broken leg, don't you?'

'Sir, only a certificate!'

'Yes, of course!'

'Yes, sir!'

'See … plastering your leg is not required. I'll write such an excuse on your medical certificate that no one will question it. You'll only require a crepe bandage.'

'Sir, but it won't produce the same effect. A plaster is much more profound.'

'I'll handle the matter if your professor questions it. Don't worry, son. I'll write that you had a ligament tear. You say you tripped on a stone. Even if one does an X-ray, a ligament tear doesn't show and is the safest. You don't worry about all that. Fine?'

'Thank you, doctor.'

'Oh, don't say that. I am pleased to help you. Now tell me your name and college,' he said and tore off a sheet from his pad.

'Sir, Tejas Narula, IIT Delhi.'

He had lowered his pen to the paper but stopped midway. He looked up at me with astonishment in his eyes. He studied me and his mouth opened wider with each passing second, like an inflating balloon.

'God, this cannot be possible!' he uttered and shook his head.

'Huh!' I uttered, almost involuntarily.

'Tell me, aren't you Ravi's son?'

I jumped from my chair and sprang a good metre or two in the air, narrowly missing the ceiling. If ever there was a line that could induce more horror in this human, I hadn't heard it – 'Tell me, aren't you Ravi's son' … hell, that is precisely who I am – Ravi's son, Dr Ravi and Dr Madhu Narula's proud son. How on earth did he know my dad's name? It was evident that my surname had rung a bell. I kept staring at him, wondering what to say.

'Tell me, boy, aren't you the son of Ravi Narula, J Batch, AFMC, Pune? You resemble him so much.'

I was speechless. I congratulated Mr Fate. If you put a black ball in a bag along with nine-ninety-nine red balls, your probability of drawing the black one is still higher than mine finding a doctor who was my father's classmate. Mr Fate had switched sides again. Little use cursing Fate, I thought, for I realised that I had been staring at the doctor for too long. What to say in response was another question that perplexed me. I could tell him he was mistaken. It would have been nice and merry, if I was indeed his pal's son, but I hated to break the news that I was not. But then he, in his suspicion, might decide to call my dad and ask him, 'Tell me, Narula, was your son in Pune?'

To which my father would reply, 'Yes!'

'He was up to something. Something dubious, I tell you,' this doctor would say and all hell would break loose.

'Yes, sir, I am his son,' I said, hoping I'd be able to persuade him not to bother my dad.

'Oh, I knew it. But tell me, what happened? Is all well at home? Your friend told me that there was a severe family crisis. Is my friend fine?'

I had forgotten all about that rotten excuse. Family crisis, indeed. What was to be done now? I kept on gaping at the doctor stupidly.

'You can tell me, son, he was a great friend at college. I feel bad that we aren't in touch, and that I couldn't help him when he was in trouble. But it seems god has sent you to bring us back together.'

There was no escaping now. There was only one way out. To tell the truth and hope for sympathy. I couldn't conjure a family problem, and assure my dad's friend that it was alright, and that he shouldn't bother.

'Uncle,' I began, 'My friend lied to you. There is no family trouble. I wanted an excuse out of this tour for another reason, and I am not sure if you will find it worthy. But I beg you not to tell my father, as that will surely lead to a family problem.'

'What is it?' he asked suspiciously and I told him all, like the way I had been forced to tell so many others. He stood up and came to my side of the table and looked at me with fatherly eyes. I saw his shoes finally. They were shining black. And so his scruples shone as bright. He looked at me dreamily and said, 'Do you really love the girl or just want to have fun?'

'Come on, uncle, I won't risk so much just to have fun.'

'True! You know, if you love her so much, you should have told your father.'

'Uncle, I didn't know how he'd take it. You know how it is with parents. I am really friendly with my dad, but...'

'He would have been proud of you, son!'

'What?' I uttered.

'Yes, it would've reminded him of his days, and he would have helped you to go and meet your love. That is how he is, your dad.'

'Really?' I asked surprised. I knew my dad was a playful lad in his days, but this was a tad too playful.

'You know what, if this helps you, your dad would have done the very thing if he were in your place,' he said, smiling.

It did help me. But then, a curious question came to my mind.

'Uncle, did my father ever do such a thing?'

He smiled. His eyes lit up and he said, 'I have told you enough, my friend. Let secrets remain buried between old timers.' I got it. My father had done something in his heydays. It may not have been spanning the country to meet his love, but something crazy, something that couldn't be told to all. I was relieved.

'So will you help me, uncle?'

'Of course,' he said smiling, 'You know, you resemble your dad in looks, and even more in disposition. I am proud of you, son. Always follow your heart.'

And with that he went back to his desk, and resumed writing the medical certificate. It was extremely gratifying to know that someone so much like my father approved of my ways. There were people in this world who understood love and that made me happy. I saluted the doctor, my father's friend.

He tied the crepe bandage neatly and firmly on my ankle, and taught me how to limp, laughing all along, and reliving his youth.

'Come, son; let us go to the professor.'

'You will come?' I asked surprised.

'Of course, I have to. Nothing must go wrong. I'll drop you personally in my car and no one will ever suspect anything.'

I looked at him appreciatively. I could never thank him enough. Here was a man I aspired to be. I wished I had told my dad too.

A question came to my lips. 'Uncle, do you, by any chance, play the harmonica?'

'Why, no, son!'

'Oh, leave it in that case.'

'Remember, whenever you tell your dad, one day you will, of course … tell him, to give me a call. I'll call him in a couple of days, oh don't worry, I'll mention nothing of this, just a li'l catching up, son. So, yes, tell him to give me a call then; he owes me one now.'

'Sure,' I said and he put his arm around my shoulder.

'Now, let us go and tell the professor what happened,' he said with child-like enthusiasm.

'Thanks a lot, uncle.'

'Oh, I should thank you, son … thank you for letting me relive my college days. Oh, what crazy, fun-filled days those were,' he said dreamily, 'And after such a long time, I am back to doing what I enjoyed most – playing around with prickly professors,' he laughed at that and added as I walked, 'Remember, son, you have a ligament tear, and a man with a ligament tear should limp.' We both emerged out of his clinic laughing, much to the surprise of my three friends who stood outside, waiting.

Mr Fate had switched sides, yet again.

ᔆ

A crowd had gathered around Ram Lodge, Junglee Maharaj Road, Pune in a vague semicircle. At the centre of it, stood seven people – a boy with a bandaged foot, supported by two loyal friends, a doctor, as was evident by the stethoscope hanging from his neck, and three others; a man, a woman and a child.

The inner crust of this crowd looked on with frank astonishment and the outer crust just looked on to see what had happened that so many people were looking on. There were two short men in this outer crust who, despite being on their toes and craning their necks, were unable to see the scene at the centre.

'What happened?' asked short man A to short man B.

'They say there was an accident,' replied B, giving up his struggle to watch the proceedings live.

'Was there blood?' asked A.

'Oh yes! A lot of it, they say a truck hit him,' said B.

'A truck, it must have been a painful sight!' said A.

'Very!' said B.

'Did you see the victim?' asked A enthusiastically.

'Yes, a young boy,' bragged B, obviously lying.

'Is he alive?' asked A.

'Probably not!' said B, coldly, and moved off, while A got on his toes again, trying to catch a glimpse, wondering about the growing callousness in the world.

Meanwhile, unaware of the mussing of the short man, I stood before the professor, his wife and Kittu, as Dr Prabhakar spoke on, 'He must have strict bed rest for at least fifteen days or it can be serious.'

The professor looked on in a sympathetic manner, just as the doctor had looked at me when I had entered his clinic. His look was even more compassionate, more like that of a mother whose child had fallen off a bicycle.

'He must have rest then,' he declared.

'It is vital,' added the doctor.

'Tej, I know you were so enthusiastic about the tour, you arranged it all and god decides to injure you out of everybody,' he said.

'Unfair,' added Dr Prabhakar.

'Most!' said the professor, 'I know you will not like this, Tej, but you must not visit any industries.' And then, looking at the doctor he said, 'He must be sad, you haven't the slightest idea how he helped arranging this tour. He is a fine boy.'

'I have gathered as much from the short acquaintance I have had with him, professor,' said the doctor. I looked on as if the world had ended. 'No tour, no life' was the message that my face flashed.

Meanwhile, the astonishment of the inner crust, which consisted of my peers, had increased to bursting point and there was absolute mayhem. The students were obviously amazed at the developments, refusing to believe it all, for it was none other than Tejas Narula at the helm of affairs.

'Sir, it is okay; I will rest. I will talk to my father and ask him what to do,' I said, hanging on to the branches that my friends offered.

'If you want to go home, do that, but make sure you are comfortable,' said the professor.

I wanted to dance but didn't. I wanted to smile but didn't. I just thanked god. The final frontier had been conquered. There was no stopping me now. I looked at my friends and then at the doctor, thanking them with my eyes. I could see that they could barely suppress their happiness too. The time had come to walk off from the scene, or rather limp off, for how long can mirth be muffled?

'Sir, I'll do that,' I said, 'I'd like to rest now.'

'By all means,' said the professor, 'And thanks a lot, doctor. Really nice of you to bring him here personally. You two, take good care of him.'

'Yes, sir,' added my friends.

'We will miss you, Tej,' said the professor. 'I'll miss you too bhaiya,' said Kittu, who had become a friend during the train journey.

'I'll miss you all too,' I said and limped off, wondering if that was correct. The professor withdrew into his quarters. The crowd started to disperse. The whole junta of Industrial and Production Engineering surrounded the three of us as we made our way. Voices could be heard, 'What the hell is this?'

'This is arbit!'

'Is this genuine, Tej?'

I remained silent, while my two friends did their best in answering their questions. I had never felt better before.

Pune Station. 13 December, that year

I sat on a bench on platform number three. It was one forty-five in the night and my train was two hours late. The station was a lonely place at that hour. A few shops were still open and a few passengers were there on the platform, but to me they were all non-existent. I was in the strangest of moods, one of those that people like to term 'philosophical'.

In my hands was a copy of *Carry On, Jeeves* but even its brilliantly humorous prose ceased to have an effect. I was supposed to be happy but I was not. My eyes were supposed to sparkle, instead they housed contemplation. I was a train journey away from my love with nothing to stop me but I did not give it a thought.

It was strange. All along my journey, though I had thoroughly enjoyed its ups and downs, I had wished to see the end of it. And now I hesitated to move ahead.

I'd miss those times. Right from the night Shreya told me she could not come, to this night, I'd miss it all – the plotting during lectures – those phone calls with Shreya – that shower of soda and the tussle with Pappi – the near inclusion in the shot-put team – my broken foot – Biobull – the many wonderful people who had helped me along the way – Vineet, Foxy, Dusky, Ria didi, Sneha, Bajrang, Dr Prabhakar …

The Chennai Express entered the station and I got busy in transferring my belongings. The train brought with itself fresh excitement and energy. The brooding look on my face slowly made way for the sparkle in my eyes. I looked out of the window at the starlit sky as the train started to move. The cool breeze flirted with my face, stirring in me, once again, bright emotions of love and victory. It was no time to brood, I told myself, but a time to remember forever. Nothing could stop me now; I was on my way.

❦

I was in the deepest of slumbers on the top berth when I heard an explosion. It took me some seconds to realise that Dusky couldn't be around and the blast I heard was no ordinary one. Sleepily, I looked right and left from my berth as the train slowed to a stop. Passengers talked among themselves nervously before an old turbaned man advised them to hush and then shouted, 'There are ghosts in these parts...'

I stretched myself and peeped below cautiously. I saw a man crouched in fear. His face was hidden in shadow.

'Hello,' I said in a whisper, hanging my head down, and at that our friend stiffened.

'Don't worry, I am not one of those ghosts he warns us about,' I resumed, clearing my credentials. It was essential to make further conversation.

'Then don't hang like that like a bat; you almost killed me!'

I moved my head and hissed, 'Do you believe in ghosts?'

'I was never sure ...'

'Care for a walk to clear your doubts?' I asked to amuse myself.

'Are you mad?'

'At least turn on the light ...'

'Why take a chance?'

There was silence. A pin-drop silence, as it is sometimes defined. There wasn't even a whisper to wake up a sleeping monster.

'Ghosts like it dark,' I resumed.

'What about hot chocolate fudge?'

'What?' I asked, pleasantly surprised at the discovery of a funny bone in my bogey-mate, and added, 'I will ask the first one I bump into …'

'Good, then shut up. I am sure they like sounds,' he whispered, as loud as one can in a whisper.

'I will if you switch on the light. I have heard it makes them tremble.'

'I have heard that too!'

'Or was it fire?'

'Yes, it was!'

'We can't be sure, I wish my mom was here. She knows all about these things.'

In the absence of a reply, I hung my head down again, which, to my satisfaction, extracted a squeal from our friend, which led to nervous whispering among our fellow bogey-mates.

'It feels so much more secure when there is talk,' I said.

'Why take a chance?' was all I got from him.

The man was incorrigible. I decided to give in. We were immersed in silence again, a deafening one this time.

❧

The deafening silence was shattered in a manner so majestic, that it would have embarrassed the metaphorical storm of the sea that breaks the calm. It seemed that a herd of wild bulls had broken loose after days of torture. The noise went higher and higher till it threatened to demolish entire aural mechanisms. Remembering the doppler effect, which spoke about the character of approaching and receding sound waves, I derived that the present wave had to be the former, and, therefore, stiffened a little and lay waiting.

The sounds kept their promise, as a barrage of men, not bulls, stormed into our bogey, and threatened to take it apart. They whizzed past me like a train within a train, and only after they had gone past me completely did I dare to look up and out of my berth.

Ghosts would have been better, bulls too, but what met the eye were policemen as lavishly decorated with guns as an Indian bride with jewellery. I craned my neck and saw that they were running after two short, bald men whose oily heads shone in the dim light of the bogey.

Hadn't I passed enough exams, I asked god at that moment, that he had to spring up rogues and cops out of nowhere to test my will? Weren't professors enough? I was cross. It wouldn't have surprised me if a gunman were to emerge out of the dark and take me as a hostage. Mr Fate's game was getting dirtier. Of all the million trains in this country, which had the second largest rail network in the world, the criminals had to choose this one!

My mind was busy cursing the latest development that threatened my trip, and calculating the zeroes after the decimal in the probability of this happening with any traveller. What if the entire train was blown up? My sister's comments came back to haunt me – What if something happens? How will I forgive myself? – as I heard several thuds and explosions in the distance. The blast that had interrupted my siesta, I now understood, was firing. The present sounds came from far off, and I was relieved that the battle scene had shifted outside.

I tried to resume my talk with the chap in the lower berth and manage a laugh in those trying times.

'Sorry, no ghosts to greet us today!' I whispered.

'Shhh ... there are crooks and bullets ...' he whispered.

'Want to have a peep outside?' I joked.

'Are you mad?'

'They must be dead!'

'Still, why take a ...'

Before he could say 'chance' the lights were switched on suddenly. I stiffened again and he crouched as we waited for hell to break loose. A stick banged against metal and a gruff voice started shouting. 'Don't worry, now,' it said in a coarse Bihari accent, 'All is safe. The bandits have been killed. The train will start soon ...'

I stuck my head out, this time without any hesitation and saw a policeman in khaki, rubbing his thumb on his palm as he spoke coolly.

✍

It was four in the morning and the nerve-shattering episode had, in addition, shattered any hopes of getting sleep. I cooed to my friend on the berth beneath, 'Are you asleep?'

'Yes, I am!' he said.

'Mind some gupshup?'

'Not a bad idea, sleep's off on a holiday,' he replied.

I was surprised. I had expected a 'why-take-a-chance'. I hopped down while he put the light on. What I saw was a pleasant surprise. The man seemed to be in his late twenties and had the air of being well-read. We shook hands.

'Hope I didn't bother you much! I have this habit of talking...'

'You had the nerve to joke around in those tense times...'

'Humour was important then ...'

'But it could have attracted danger, my friend.'

'You really believe in ghosts?'

'Those outlaws were no less dangerous. By the way, I am Rajit Rajit Ahuja!'

'I am Bond,' I laughed, 'No poor jokes, I am Tejas Narula.'

'So what do you do?'

'I am studying at IIT Delhi,' I replied.

Suddenly his eyes lit up and his face beamed. Never had the name of my college made someone so plump with joy. His face had the look of a proud father whose son had just got into IIT.

'Unbelievable,' he exclaimed and that disappointed me.

'I know, I don't look like one from …'

'Oh, no, it is not that, bhai.' This was the first time he had addressed me as 'bhai' and his forthcoming words explained why. 'I too am from IIT.'

It is a thing well documented about IITians that when two of the same species meet, no matter which year they passed out, or which of the seven renowned institutions they belonged to, they look upon each other as long lost brothers. The eye is one of affection and the heart one of warmth.

He discovered the tone and idiom of yesteryears before he could blink an eye. He was from IIT-B. Which dep (department)? *Batti* (Electrical). He passed out four years back, enriched his curriculum vitae with a degree from IIM Bangalore, and now worked in Pune.

'What takes you to Chennai, bro?' I asked.

He smiled slightly and blushed a bit. There was an unmistakable glimmer in his eyes and I got it.

'I'm getting married, yaar.'

'Congratulations! Love or arranged?' I asked – the first question that pops into one's head when one talks about marriage.

'You won't believe it, my story! It is a one in a million case.'

I frowned. 'Is it a boy?'

'No, come on!'

'Then, tell me all.'

'You know what; Nivedita and I were at school together. Nivedita, that's her.'

'I thought as much, go on.'

'My dad got transferred to Chennai when I was in the eleventh and we fell in love.'

'Great, it has been long!'

'Nine years!'

'That's a double PhD. in love. So, when did you break it to your folks?'

'The answer will boost your belief in god.' I raised an eyebrow, just one. 'You know what, she is south Indian. And her dad is a professor at IIT Madras.'

'Then he must be impressed with you.'

'No, no ... The man is a frust; comes from a school that says – Love is a pest, and papa knows best.'

'Then?' I asked. He had all my attention. His case was not dissimilar to mine, and was about to have a happy ending.

'You won't believe it, just when she and I were wondering how to put it across to him, a marriage proposal came to my place.'

'Then? You surely tore it up!'

'Exactly! That was my first impulse. I told mom I'd have nothing to do with proposals. I hate them.'

'So do I.'

'So I told her to tear the photo to shreds. But she somehow convinced me that the *bandi* was a bomb and deserved a look.'

'She said that? Your mom's a sport.'

'Oh, no. I meant beautiful.'

'You looked at it? No fight in looking at pretty faces...'

'Exactly ...'

'Yes, then?'

'The roof fell over my head and the ground escaped from beneath my feet. It was her.'

'Who?'

'Nivedita!'

'Who?'

'That's her.'

'The bomb?'

He eyed me and I sank back into my seat like a boneless mammal. I understood now why his case was one in a million. Make it one in a billion. Add it to the wonders of the world list. Declare him the luckiest man on this planet. I shuddered to compare my life with his. He sure was the son of fortune. A thought that often comes to my mind when hearing of love stories other than mine flitted through my head – if only my life was that uncomplicated.

'What happened to you, Tejas?'

'Her parents never got a whiff of it? For nine whole years?' asked incredulously.

'No, we played it really safe and don't intend to tell him even now. I wonder how he'll react! Why take a chance?'

The man had proven his theory of life and how. It was as solid a proof as the time one that dropped into Dr Newton's head when he saw an apple fall and discovered gravity. I felt bad thinking about how I had made fun of this genius of a man, and his why-take-a-chance motto. Chicken-hearted he might be, but it had served him well. looked at him with newfound respect. He had evaded the attention of his future father-in-law for nine years while I had barely managed.

'Will you mind telling me what happened?' he asked again, 'You seem to be suffering from jaundice all of a sudden.'

I mustered all my courage to speak. 'Do you know what takes me to Chennai?'

'I am not much of a fortune teller.'

'Then let me tell you. You'd be glad to know that my story is very similar to yours except that there is a slight difference – her dad knows, and I blame it all on you. If only you had met me before, oh wise one! If only ...'

And I narrated my love story yet again. He said he understood my pain and position, but warned me that I was taking a huge chance by going to meet my beloved. He added that it was worth it now that her father wouldn't let her meet me otherwise.

'You must come to the wedding, Tejas, only if you can spare time from your dates,' he said.

'Oh, I definitely will, I'll meet her only during the day. You know how it is with girls when it comes to sneaking out of home at night.'

'Yes, especially with Nivedita; her father is a fighter. You know how profs are! He has such sidey ideas. Sample this. The dates of all the functions had been decided long back but just a week before the marriage, this man gets an arbit brainwave.'

'What?'

'The marriage is next Sunday and only yesterday he announces that a pooja must be organised!'

'I don't prefer them much either; god's everywhere; but it's not that big a fight – a small pooja!'

'Small? Your head will burst when I tell you about it. The pooja is to take place somewhere in Mahabalipuram, not for one-two hours, but spread over three days!'

'Three days?'

'Three days! The dad says it is imperative for our future!'

'What fart! These superstitions murder you!'

'And to receive such a shock out of the blue drives me to depression. You see, I am a man who likes to enjoy his holiday. I decided to travel by train because I love it. I cherish life's small joys and this man kills them. I was all geared up to have fun with my family, when this man comes up with this max arbit plan and stabs me!'

'Like he stabbed you in the middle of a sound sleep.'

I sympathised with him. Being a victim of the whims and fantasies of a girl's father myself, I could understand what he felt. If there is a man, whom to avoid you'd give any price, it is a girl's father. Your girl's, of course. I gave Mr Rajit a friendly pat.

'Don't worry, my friend, it'll all be fine. It's only a picnic of three days!'

'Oh, I don't know what I'll do,' he almost cried, 'The only solace is that I'll have my sister there. Oh, that reminds me … the last time I talked to her, Shreya didn't sound alright. She said there was something important …'

'Who didn't sound alright?' I asked. I was half dead.

'My sister.'

'I mean, what is her name?'

'Shreya, why?' That completed the murder. Rajit Ahuja also known as Shreya's 'Raju bhaiya' – the one who used to carry her piggyback all day long – the very brother who was getting married. I wondered what prevented her from calling him 'Rajit bhaiya' and cursed the Indian tradition of keeping pet names. I closed my eyes and fell back into my seat. It didn't seem like a seat at all, but like a pit a million miles deep. Even if that ol' harmonica buzzed at that point, I hadn't the capacity to notice. Numb, that is what they call it, I was.

❧

The train had assumed what must have been its fastest pace after the shock of the discovery of bandits on its frame. Most of the people had succeeded in their attempts to beat the demons out of their heads, and had gone off to sleep.

However, in the darkness, a singular light shone and illuminated the bogey S-4. A photosensitive traveller, had he got up to inflict upon the illuminator a what-the-hell-are-you-doing-at-five-in-the-night speech, would have seen two pale faces – paler in the yellow light of the train – looking at each other dumbly like ducks. In reality, nobody came and disturbed the ducks. They were alone in their compartment, which usually gets filled along the journey and, from the look on their faces, it seemed they were in the middle of what is called an awkward moment.

I, as one of the ducks, can tell you for sure that I didn't have a clue about what to say and my brother-in-law wasn't doing any better. Presently he closed his eyes, trying to gulp in the shocking news. A lump the size of a basketball appeared in the middle of his throat. I couldn't blame him for his reaction. I empathised with the poor soul. Of all the shockers, if there is one that sends the chilliest of chills down your spine, it is the one that deals with the discovery of your darling sister's darling.

'When did she grow so old?' is a question that every brother asks himself, wondering at the ways of nature – so fast, so furious. Till yesterday, the cute little girl was this high, he says to himself pointing to his knees, and has now become big enough to fall in love! Years flash by so fast, he reflects, and curses them. A brother doesn't like to hear from his sister, 'My dear brother, you yourself are in love!'

The brother doesn't see any sense in this parallel. 'Don't give my example,' he says, 'I am wise. You are an innocent girl and any guy can fool you!

Anyhow, I didn't know whether to feel unlucky or lucky. A part of me called Mr Fate names like I so often had during the journey.

In desperation, Mr Fate had finally switched strategies and now concentrated on Shreya's end. Cheap tactics, I tell you, to worry a delicate girl. Unchivalrous, to put the poor girl at her wits end, by conjuring up, out of the blue, this whole pooja business. My darling must've been busy with her dress rehearsal, already in a muddle whether to choose the blue salwar-kameez or the pink skirt to wear on the first day, when the news must have arrived. Her sweetheart was coming to meet her, traversing the length of the country, encountering the roughest of storms, and here she was, helpless, about to be exported to some foreign land. My heart went out to her. She probably would have fainted upon hearing this. My phone was not reachable for most of the time during the trip, rendering a conversation impossible. Oh, how she would have coped with it! 'Take me on, Fate, man to man, but stop harassing my little girl!' was what I wanted to shout out.

But a second voice told the first to calm down. After all, wasn't it Fate that had placed me and the hero of the very show which might have prevented me from meeting my darling in the same compartment? The use of the word 'might' here may look like a solecism but I assure you it is not. I use the word 'might' for the pooja might have foiled my plans, but now that I knew about it, it'd be a different script. I was going to meet Shreya, if not in Chennai, then in Mahabalipuram or, for that matter, in Timbuktu, which not many people know is a place in northern Mali, Africa.

Therefore, this wise voice told me not to curse Fate, but instead to look at the brighter side of life – something I want you to remember from my story. If this man hadn't been planted below my berth by Fate, I would have waited for Shreya outside IIT Madras where we were supposed to meet, peeping desperately into passing autos, only to find no one like her in them. Mr Fate, though, had ruined quite a lot, and was also doing his best to resurrect it all. Once again I went into a pensive mode, thinking about the past and deriving hope from it. Numerous times along the journey everything had been shattered, and each time one saw the hand of Fate. But at all those times, hadn't he, not without my efforts, changed sides, proven himself an ally, and put all the pieces together? One needs perseverance and effort at all times in life. 'Buck up', one needs to say to oneself, 'and think.'

In the present dilemma, however, not much thinking was required. The only man who could help me meet Shreya sat right before me. I looked at him once again. He still looked pale; his eyes were closed, but his breathing was getting back to normal. I decided to break the silence. I put a comforting hand on his shoulder and he opened his eyes. What he saw must've been eyes full of pity and prayers.

'I know how it feels, brother. I have a sister too,' I fumbled with my opening lines. He kept looking at me unbelievingly. He didn't speak.

'I really love your sister. That is the only assurance I can offer you right now,' I added. He was still silent.

'I hope you understand, Rajit.' He kept on looking ahead in mute silence. I didn't know what to do. He had to understand; if love was a crime he himself was a criminal.

'You are the only one who can help us!' At that, he straightened himself and moved his eyes, surveying me from top to bottom.

'Not bad!' he declared at the end of it, reminding me of his sweet sister, and smiled. 'You know what, you look like a school kid,' he said, a little disapprovingly, I thought. 'But,' my friend added, 'That is good, as Shreya resembles a tenth grade girl. You'll look good together.' He smiled again, and I managed a small one too, relieved at the positive assessment.

'I am happy for her. You really love her, yaar! Stay that way always, I tell you, or else I'll break your legs,' he said, with forced menace in his voice.

'Break them, do whatever you want to but, right now, help me. Your sasurji has messed it all, both for you and me. I have to meet Shreya! At any cost!' I prayed.

'I wish I could cancel the pooja!'

'Can't you?'

'Not until the old pig-head is there.'

'Can't we do something about him?' I asked in a sinister tone.

'I'd love to do many things to him, if only Nivedita didn't love the buffoon so much …' he said in frustration, like a police officer who has been ordered to bring the gangster back alive, and only alive. Oh, how much he'd want to cut him up, but the bloody authorities hold him back.

'But something needs to be done …' I said.

'Now I see why Shreya was so worried yesterday when I talked to her. She said there was something important she wanted to tell me but her father arrived right then …'

'We should call her right away from the next station,' I said, looking at my network-less mobile phone.

'At five in the morning?'

'She'll be awake, I am sure,' I said.

'I am sure too,' Rajit smiled, 'Reminds me of old times … waiting the whole night by the phone … just for one call! Anyhow, what we should worry about right now is how to get you to Shreya!'

'Point!'

'How, how, how …' he said meditating.

'Why did god have to give me this school-kid face, I can't even play your friend.'

Just then the train whistled and began to slow down. I looked at my new friend and he looked at me, and we both shot towards the door and looked outside. It was a station. It looked like a deserted island save for a single bulb that lent its light to a tea stall. The whole station was just about the length of our train. There were hardly three or four people on the platform. Our train stopped and we both jumped out, and dashed toward the tea stall. A man sat there smoking *beedi*, wrapped in a shawl, but there was no sign of a phone there. My heart sank.

Rajit asked the stall owner, 'Any telephone booth here?' The owner looked at us suspiciously, and then like a magician, produced from behind him a bruised and battered phone.

'No meter sahib, will charge ten rupees per minute as per my watch, and you better call quick; the train will start soon, it is three hours late,' he said, coughing, and lifted his wrist to look at his watch. I dialled the number quickly and waited. Nothing happened. I dialled again. I was punching in all the wrong keys in excitement.

Rajit took the receiver from my hand. He dialled the number. I waited, keenly studying his face to spot any sign of success. 'It is ringing,' he said triumphantly and I heaved a sigh of relief. He thrust the receiver against my ear. She picked up the phone.

'Hello ...'

'Oh thank god you called, Tej, I have been calling you since yesterday, but your network ...' and she broke down.

'Don't cry, Shreya, don't cry!'

'You don't know what has happened!'

'I know. I know it all; you stop crying. I know you have to go to Mahabalipuram.'

'How do you know?' she asked surprised, still crying.

'Your very own Sherlock Holmes ...'

'Oh shut up, tell me!'

'Don't have time, Shreya, the train will start any time. Don't cry and be strong. Don't worry, I'll meet you; it'll all be fine. All this messing up is important for our tale. How else will it be interesting? So just enjoy the story that we'll tell our grandchildren ...'

'But will you tell me ... how'll you come?' she asked and at that I gave the receiver to her brother.

'Hello,' he said, 'Yes, it's me, sis, can you believe it? With Tejas ... god is great, sis, now don't worry, we'll chalk out a plan ... but wait till I get there ... I'll see you ... you didn't tell your dearest brother anything about your extremely entertaining love story ... after all the tales that he used to tell you ... disappointing ...'

The train began to move. I fished around inside my pocket for money. A hundred rupee note came into my hand. I signalled for Rajit to hang up. He handed the receiver to me.

'Okay, bye, Shreya. Didn't I tell you that I am on my way? And so I am, more than ever; just wait for me and I'll be there soon, clutching you in my arms and ... and right now I hate to hang up but the train is picking up pace. Oh, how much I love running after trains. Done that for ages. It is ... what's that word you use in college?'

'Are you mad? Get going, quick ...'

'Not until you say it.'

'Fundoolicious.'

'Oh, how utterly fundoolicious! Love you, bye ...'

'Love you too, and get in safely,' she said.

'Anything for you, ma'am,' I said and hung up. I pushed the hundred rupee note in the stall owner's hand and ran with Rajit, shouting, 'Keep the change ...' The call was priceless.

Still 13 December, that year. Morning

It was nearly eleven when I woke up. Our train was about four hours late and approached station Wadi. I hopped down with my toothbrush and soap, and made my way to the wash-basin. Meanwhile, the train had started losing pace and finally stopped. I got out.

A busy station, as we all know, is a splash of colours, and presently on this canvas a particular Sardarji stood out. His colours, by which I refer to the colour of his clothes, struck my eyes like a ball of fire. He was busy haggling with the owner of a bookshop some fifteen meters away with his back to me. He wore a red turban of the richest red, a green shirt of the richest green, and brown trousers, needless to say, of the richest brown. In short he looked like an apple tree and a drunkard could not be blamed for attempting to pluck, what he thought, must be an apple. That no drunkard was in his vicinity was a thing that our Sardarji must be thankful for.

With my eyes fixed on the human kaleidoscope, I asked the vendor for a cold-drink, and while he produced one, I saw the Sardarji try to slip his wallet into his trousers' back pocket. Well, at least our Sardarji intended to, only he didn't quite succeed. Sardarji, one saw, was extremely busy reading the book he had purchased, which he held in his left hand. What Sherlock Holmes would have deduced, had he been there, was that our man, no doubt a keen reader, was also a fastidious fellow who wouldn't like to take the time to go from the book stall to the train by mere walking. He'd have also labelled our Sardarji absent-minded, for his wallet instead of going smoothly into his pocket, went smoothly out, and hit the ground with a thud which was lost in the din of the station.

A naughty breeze, precisely a nanosecond later, encouraged a stray newspaper page to fly and land on top of the wallet. I marvelled at the scene, constructed carefully by the forces of nature. But having always been exhorted by my mum to help fellow brothers, I didn't stand sightseeing for long, and called out to the human palette, who had turned left towards the train with the book still in his left hand and a fat black trunk in his right.

There comes a stage in one's life, sooner or later, when the goriest of horrors ceases to make an impact. The ground remains firmly beneath him and the tummy bears it all without inviting butterflies. Any lesser man, had he been in my place, would have fainted right then. But what this journey of mine had done, if I could put my finger on a single thing, was turn my nerves to steel and muscles to iron. I had been surprised when dealing with the previous shockers, but to this one I turned a blind eye.

But prior to that, as Professor P.P. Sidhu looked hither and thither for the caller, the first thing to do was to take an about turn, the ones they taught us so well at school in the morning drills. I hated them back then, but at that moment a wave of appreciation swept over me. How well the school trained one to face any situation! I shifted my weight to the left foot and did a neat one-eighty-degree that would have made the fussiest of brigadiers proud.

Pappi was headed, we all remember, towards Chennai alright, but what was this detour about? I walked straight nonchalantly and hid at a vantage point behind the cold-drink shop from where I could scrutinise his movements.

◦

Lying in ambush, I saw Pappi, after his initial puzzlement at the call, proceed towards the train. He was lost in his book once more and moved slowly, always in danger of bumping into the scurrying passengers. The train rested at the station for a good fifteen minutes and Pappi took all the time in the world to reach his seat. When he was out of the danger area, I quickly moved to the book shop, and there, after letting a coin drop inconspicuously, bent and picked up the wallet along with the coin.

I flipped open the wallet and a jovial Pappi smiled at me from the right compartment. No doubt, the picture was from an age when he hadn't rubbed shoulders with me. I felt a strange empathy for him when looking at his innocent face. All his actions could be justified. He was after all, soaked in what he thought was alcohol. For the first time I felt I was not on a vengeance spree against him. Outside the walls of IIT, it is a different life. Outside his station, a policeman meets his prisoner without the same harshness.

It was no time to philosophise but to do something. I searched the wallet. There were a few hundred rupee notes, some visiting cards and the ticket. We were travelling in the same train. I looked down and could hardly believe my eyes. I didn't shout, didn't flinch; just pursed my lips and knitted my brows. It was a waitlisted ticket. Bogey S-4, seat number 43 was written by the TT on his ticket. Bogey S-4, seat number 44 was printed on mine.

⚭

I moved carefully to the window of my compartment. I quickly passed by it and a fleeting glance showed me that Pappi was busy with his trunk. I turned and trotted to the window again, and from the left corner, the one closer to Rajit, waved my right hand while my left was engaged in putting a finger on my lips – a warning for Rajit: 'Don't react!'

He was reading and noticed me after about five seconds. He was taken aback to see me in the avatar of an asylum runaway – with my eyes wide open and my hand signalling frantically – trying to tell him to come out. He, no doubt, was about to utter, 'Have you gone mad?' when, sensing that he would, I withdrew my waving right hand and employed it in unison with the left. Two fingers were probably better than one on the lips, I thought, and it did the trick.

He didn't speak but kept staring at me mutely, probably wondering what his sister saw in this boy, who went mad on serene mornings. I signalled to him to come out of the train again, and having no other option, he did so.

'Have you gone nuts?'

'No. I wanted you to come out but couldn't speak!'

'You are speaking well enough now ...'

'I mean I couldn't speak there.'

'Why?'

'Hell has broken loose ...'

'What?'

'That man in there, in our compartment, on the berth below mine and above yours is that professor from IIT Delhi ...'

'A professor!' he said in excitement as if a reunion of IITians was in progress.

'The professor ...'

'What difference does that make? How wonderful that three IITians should be in one compartment...'

'If only you'd let me complete what I'm saying.'

'Go on.'

'He is the very professor,' I explained to him, 'Professor Pappi, I told you about, who was soaked in soda by my friend and who tried everything to stop me from meeting your sister.'

And then it dawned on him. His eyes bore no more excitement but incredulity and horror. And then he spoke, spotting an anomaly, 'But you said that he had been removed.'

'I forgot to mention that he too was headed for Chennai to attend a marriage ...'

'Yes, it's this season, you know ...'

'The season can go and ... all I know is that he is right here, under my berth, like a carefully planted time bomb!'

'What is to be done?' he asked. I had a plan. The journey had trained me to think on my feet.

'I have his wallet,' I said with pride.

'Whose wallet?'

'The professor's wallet, of course! How can someone else's wallets help us?' I said irritated.

'You have his wallet,' my friend said calmly. But presently his eyes sported a look of disapproval.

'Yes, here it is.' I showed him.

'Rotten!' he said shaking his head.

'I know, battered old wallet, torn at places, leather's cracking and fading. Calls for a change. An ideal birthday gift for ...'

'I didn't mean the wallet...'

'Then?' I asked perplexed.

'You had the cheek to put your hand in his ...' and at that he shook his head again, wondering whether his sister ought to be allowed to continue her romance with a pickpocket. I pondered over the insanity of the notion.

'Do I look like a dacoit?' I demanded indignantly, though fearing that he might say 'yes'.

'Where did you get it from?' he asked and I described the beautiful scene to him.

'Ah,' he said, satisfied.

'Now, listen. You go into the bogey and somehow take the Prof. away from our berths. Meanwhile, I will sneak in and climb onto my berth, turn my head towards the other side, crouch and lie there. Then he won't be able to see me.'

He listened intently but saw something amiss. 'How will that help you?'

'He won't know that I am there.'

'Let me put it this way. Won't you ever feel the need to urinate? How on earth will we plan this?'

'I haven't finished, my friend; you forget the wallet,' I said waving it.

'What about it?'

'You know what is in it?'

'Money.'

'And?'

'The photo of his wife and kids ...'

'And?'

'Stop farting. I know what a wallet contains.'

'But you miss the nub of the story. What must the wallet of a train passenger contain?'

His eyes were now the eyes of an able conspirator. He saw it all now. 'His ticket,' he said, moving his head slowly up and down.

'And what does that make him, comrade?' I asked. I felt like one of those rebels hatching a plan to bomb the president's car.

'A ticket-less traveller!'

'You are right, comrade, but to be more general, what does that make him in the eyes of law?'

'A criminal,' he said, and I couldn't have used a better word.

'A criminal, a law-breaker, a person, comrade, who, the law clearly states, can be sentenced to a good time in jail or imposed a good fine, the amount of which I do not recall.'

'Neither do I.'

'Immaterial. The nub again is that our criminal neither has the ticket nor the money to save his good self.' My partner in crime looked at me with eyes of appreciation. Fit, he probably felt, is this boy for my sister.

'So when the ticket-collector is about to arrest him for his offence and send him off to keep murderers and pickpockets company, I'll save him the humiliation by descending down from my berth like god's messiah incarnate, correcting the TT that the man he looks upon as a swine from behind his spectacles, is actually my respected guru from IIT Delhi accompanying me on a technical project. I'll then pay off his fine, thus becoming a ...'

'Hero in his eyes ...'

'Exactly, a hero, god's messenger, an angel of humanity ... And then he'll have no option but to be grateful to me and bury the past. Of course I'll tell him that I was not involved in the least in that shower incident and that I don't even drink, and he will no doubt understand!'

'Faadu! Genius! Hey, but will he not ask you, what you are doing in this train?'

'He will.'

'What'll you tell him?'

I opened the wallet and showed him Pappi's photo. 'Don't you think he is a nice man? Just look at his eyes!'

'Yes, I talked to him ... seemed a pleasant fellow.'

'And a pleasant fellow he is! He was angry with me only because he thought I insulted him. But after I clear his doubts, he will be a darling again. Don't you think such a man, touched by my act of deliverance, will understand my story?'

'Maybe.'

'I think he will. After all, a professor ceases to be a professor outside the four walls of his college. Just like a policeman ceases to be a policeman outside his beat. Society teaches us to play these dual roles, my friend. A professor he might be, but when not delivering a lecture, when not marking papers; he becomes just another human being – a father, a husband, and a friend. He is an average human right now – a man who reads novels, listens to music, likes to joke; a man vulnerable to emotions. Of course some men are brutes, but look at him. Does he look like one of those? You get what I mean?'

'Best of luck! God, you speak too much!'

✎

It had been a good two hours. Two hours and no TT! Initially, when I was feeling fresh, I felt like a tiger ready to pounce on its prey. But now as time tiredly trudged past, I was reminded of a frustrating 'hide and seek' game I had once been involved in. I had hid in a similar awkward position, in the cupboard of a reeky attic, and the 'denner', as it is called, never turned up.

I wanted to sleep but couldn't afford to. The arrival of the TT couldn't be missed. There hadn't been much talk between Rajit and Pappi. They were both busy reading. 'Ticket please,' I heard faintly and a wave of fresh energy swept my body.

I produced my ticket from above without getting noticed by Pappi who was busy searching for his. The TT had a red tikka smeared on his forehead. His glasses balanced themselves on the very tip of his nose, above which his eyes looked piercingly at our professor, waiting for him to produce his ticket. I couldn't help looking at the professor sitting opposite restlessly checking all his pockets for his wallet. 'Just a second, sir, I might have dropped it,' he said to the TT as he bent down and looked underneath.

'I know where your wallet is, mister,' the TT said suspiciously.

'You are mistaken, sir, I am a ...' and then suddenly the professor's eyes lit up. Hope was back. 'Sir,' he said to the TT, 'I might have kept it in my trunk, let me check.'

Horror filled the TT's eyes and he shouted, 'Wait!' A man from the pantry had stopped to watch the entertaining scene and the TT ordered him, 'Hold him! Hold him tight, don't let him move, I'll be back!' He lifted Pappi's trunk and rushed off.

Where had the TT gone? To get a challan slip? But why with the trunk? Pappi offered no resistance, yet the man held on to him as if he was a mass of sand. I braced myself to descend as the TT approached us and told myself, 'Here you go!'

But I had to stop. Behind the TT were two policemen and a hawaldar. The petty offence surely didn't require three of the police force. One of them looked at Pappi in a ruthless manner. The professor opened his mouth to speak but before he could, the policeman spoke, 'Welcome, Mansukh Lal, after all these years, what a brilliant disguise but what a foolish mistake ...'

The frightened look on Pappi's face turned to a confused one. What on earth was the policeman talking about? Who the dickens was Mansukh Lal? And what the devil was a brilliant disguise?

'Sir, you are mistaken, I am not Mansukh Lal, I am Professor Prabjot Pal Sidhu, a professor at IIT Delhi and I have lost my wallet. I want to search my trunk for it, but the TT ...'

The policeman laughed loudly and his subordinates joined in too. 'Ha-ha, ha-ha,' the voices roared in our bogey. The policeman banged his truncheon against metal and it was all dead serious again.

'Look into your trunk indeed! No use, Mansukh, dodging me! Ten years! Ten years, it took to close in on you and your gang. And you want me to allow you to open your filthy trunk, take out your pistol and run away again, you scoundrel! I had alerted all the officials to report to me in case of any suspicion. I knew I'd catch you the moment we shot two of your gang and wasn't I right? You are under arrest!'

Gone was the look of apology in Pappi's eyes for not producing his ticket. 'Ticket-less' they might insult him with, but certainly not with 'scoundrel'. He was a man of dignity. There was a change, meanwhile, in my plan. I couldn't descend and tell the officer that he was my professor. The police would want proof and the wallet would have to be produced. I had to wait for the moment when I could plant it somewhere.

'Excuse me, officer,' said Pappi, 'You are mistaken. I told you I am not Mansukh, and I will have no more insults. I am a professor and demand due respect. What proof do you have that I am Mansukh?'

'Proof, indeed!' shouted the officer, 'You think you can dress like a Sardarji and get away. I appreciate your genius, but by losing your ticket you have committed a folly. Hawaldar,' he addressed his subordinate, 'Tear off his beard!'

Rajit jumped out of his berth and shook me hard. I had turned into a statue. 'Shoot, before they do,' he said seconds after Pappi was taken away.

I ran after them.

Flashing the wallet in my hand, I shouted, 'Wait!' They all stopped. The professor's beard was in place and I thanked god. Pappi looked at me in disbelief. The officer shouted back, 'What?' I moved towards them and then asked Pappi, 'Is this your wallet?' His eyes lit up as he cried, 'Yes!' He showed them the ticket and his I-card, and then noted their names in a pocket diary.

≈

'Okay, okay,' he said drawing a deep breath. I had told him about the real sequence of events that transpired on the soda-shower night.

The nasality of his 'okay(s)' suggested that he was almost satisfied. 'In any case I am not your professor here, just a fellow passenger. Besides you saved my life today ... I will ask you in a moment, Tejas, but what takes you to Madras, Rajit?'

I answered excitedly, 'Sir, it's his marriage; been in love for nine years!'

'Congratulations, son! That's a coincidence, I am also going for a wedding.' We knew that.

He looked at me then, and spotting kindness in his eyes, I began, 'Sir, I'll tell you the truth. I hope you don't punish me.'

'You told me your brother was getting married ...'

'I lied to you ...'

'Then tell me the truth.'

'Sir, I don't know what to say ...'

'You love someone?' he asked, so coolly, that it startled me. Perhaps he himself had been a victim once. I merely nodded my head.

'You don't have to be afraid. Treat me as your friend. Why are you going to Chennai?'

I told him the whole story in brief. It was odd talking to a professor about love. I was beginning to see the human side of my teacher now.

'It is unfair that you have to meet your friend in this fashion,' he said at the end of it and smiled genially.

'Sir, I hope you understand.'

'I understand there is more to life than industrial visits.'

'Sir, what about Biobull?' I hastened to change the topic.

'Oh, the project is almost complete. One purpose of going to Chennai is to test it!' I remembered what Vineet had told me about his collaborator. 'You see, two of us are working on the project. My partner is a professor in IIT Madras. We've been working as a team.

We decided to make two buses, one in Chennai and one in Delhi. There are still some issues at my end, but this man is ready with a prototype.'

'So, you are going for both the bus and the wedding?'

He laughed. 'Oh, you can say that they are one and the same. You see, Mr Iyer is a crazy man, but we have become friends working together ...'

He had to stop. Our friend Rajit had uttered a squeal. His eyes threatened to pop out of his sockets and he coughed with such force that his lungs were in danger of coming out through his mouth. He drank some water and spoke in a hoarse voice,

'What was the name you said, Professor Sidhu?'

'Mr Iyer, Anant Iyer. Why what happened?'

'Yes, what happened?' I asked too.

'The three of us are going to the same destination. Mr Iyer is my father-in-law!'

'What!' said the professor.

'What!' said I, and sank back into my seat again. Pappi had a partner in IIT Madras. The partner was Rajit's father-in-law and Rajit was Shreya's brother. Shreya, who of course is my love. It completed the circle. It was all as if a jigsaw puzzle had been carefully constructed by Mr Fate, and only now the pieces were falling in place. An invisible thread had linked us right from the beginning of the journey, only now it made itself visible. But then that is life.

During the journey, everything peculiar had happened for a reason. This new revelation, I was sure, had one too. I was on my feet in a flash with tremendous excitement.

'Sir, you said that the bus and the wedding are one and the same. Why?' I asked.

'Oh, you see, Mr Iyer wants to inaugurate the bus on the occasion of his daughter's marriage. Thinks it is auspicious. So he has this insane idea that the bus, on its first drive, should carry the whole marriage party and go to Mahabalipuram for a pooja he is conducting. You must be aware of it. The pooja will serve two purposes, he says, it will bless the wedding and the bus. He is a little crazy ... told me about the plan only three days back, and hasn't told anyone in his family; says it is a surprise, a wedding gift for his daughter. So, Rajit, don't tell her about this. Okay?'

'Yes!' shouted a voice. It was not Rajit's approval but a yelp from me. I had found a way.

'What happened?' asked my fellow IITians.

'Sir, I didn't tell you everything about the trip. This extremely long and taxing trip was on the verge of being decimated. And I'll tell you why! This Mr Iyer of yours is indeed a crazy man, slightly insane if I may say so in front of you!'

'Alright with me, but is it with him?' he said, pointing to Rajit.

'Oh sir, he cannot agree more. So this sudden plan of his, his obnoxious habit of springing surprises ...'

'On early mornings ...' added Rajit.

'On early mornings,' I repeated, 'this must be taken into account ...'

'And in tight times ...' added Pappi.

'And in tight times,' I added, 'No doubt put you both off, wrecked your mental peace, and for that he must not be spared; but for me, sir, he spun the most distressing predicament.'

'What?' asked Pappi.

'Don't you get it, sir, by arranging this sudden pooja, he transported Shreya like a black magician from Chennai to Mahabalipuram!'

'Who is Shreya?' he asked absent-mindedly.

'Sir, my ...' I said blushing.

'Oh, I get it, but why is she going to Mahabalipuram?'

'For the pooja, sir!'

'Why should she go for the pooja?' he asked incredulously.

At first I thought it was his absent-mindedness in full form. But then I realised I hadn't apprised him of a crucial fact.

'She is my sister!' it was not me, of course, but Rajit who said that, and the professor had his circle of coincidences complete. He uttered a squeal similar to that of Rajit and fell back, unable to digest any more.

'Sir,' I began, 'You must muster all your energy and excitement as you are the only one who can help me! I know the mystifying chains of providence have taken a toll on you, as on both of us, but you must help me!'

'Oh, you speak too much, Tejas,' he said feebly, 'How?'

'You said that everyone will go to Mahabalipuram in the same bus!'

'Yes.'

'So you must take me along too, as an assistant student who has worked closely with you on this project, and who you thought must be there for the first drive.'

'Is there no other way?' he asked.

'No sir!'

'Fine,' he said, 'Don't worry!' and at that I gave another yelp and hugged my favourite professor. He was a gem indeed. And then Rajit hugged me. It was a time to celebrate. What a journey it had been! Professor P. P. Sidhu had come full circle from being a darling to my doom to a darling again! How much I used to curse Biobull in the project days, but how it had saved me, time and again! Only Mr Fate could pull that off and, presently, I hailed him and prayed for him to remain my ally for some more days.

'Which one of you plays the guitar?' asked Pappi, seeing it lying on the top berth.

'I do, sir.'

'Then bring it down. I have a song for the occasion. The music will help restore my nervous system.'

'Mine too,' added Rajit.

As I began strumming the chords, Pappi interrupted me. 'Wait!' he said, 'Wait a while, son!' He lifted his trunk, opened it, and produced a harmonica.

You could have knocked me down with a feather. I kept on goggling at my respected Professor and then winked involuntarily. Only he didn't reciprocate and said, 'What was that, Tejas. Do you mind?' as he put the instrument to his lips.

'No, sir!'

Thus the band started – Professor on the harmonica, Tejas on the guitar, and Rajit on the tabla that he played against the train wall. The train rattled and swayed on, brimming with joy and excitement. And the compartment with the three generations of IITians made the maximum noise.

🠒

I looked out of the window. Both my friends had slept off. The compartment now had other passengers too. I watched as the meadows and farms rushed past. Nothing provides a more complete panorama of India as the window of a train does. And of course looking out of the window has other advantages. It tells you that you are getting closer and closer to your love.

Chennai. 14 December, that year

The driver inserted the key while Professor Sidhu, Professor Iyer and Professor, excuse me, Tej, just Tej looked over his shoulder. The coconut had been smashed, a quick prayer said by a group of teachers and students, and the shining green Biobull smeared with a vermillion tilak.

'Turn the key slowly, Pandey,' said Prof. Iyer to the driver, closing his eyes and remembering god. Pandey turned the key. The engine roared and roared and then went 'Phussss …'

My heart sank, 'Not another problem now!' Biobull, besides existing for my good, was of significance for the nation. Finally the dreams of alternate fuel were being realised. I prayed quietly and so did the other two professors.

'I told you to go slow, Pandey,' rebuked Mr Iyer.

He took charge himself. He turned the key as gently as one could and the engine roared again, and this time went on and on. Pandey pushed the accelerator, the engine roared more, and then he put the bus into gear. The bus started moving! It was a success. A landmark! The professors hugged each other and then hugged me in that moment of glory.

We were on our way. We emerged out of IIT Madras, which is a picturesque leafy place, to pick up the other family members. We were to meet them at a shrine on a beach adjacent to ECR, the

East Coast Road. After Dr Iyer's surprise, the party would proceed to Mahabalipuram in Biobull. There were limited guests which included, of course, my friend Rajit and his pretty sister Shreya. It was a simple wedding and only close relatives had been invited. I had been successfully introduced as Professor P.P. Sidhu's favourite student and added to the party.

Biobull, in spite of all its advantages, had a major drawback. The professors had ordered Pandey not to exceed the speed of twenty kph. At that restless hour you could not have satisfied me with a speed of hundred, and, watching rickshaws and cycles overtake the bus, I felt like jumping out and running to my love. 'You have waited for six months, sixty minutes more will not kill you,' I told myself.

Once clear of traffic, the journey on East Coast Road was delightful. The road went straight and wide, splitting the sea. The bus turned left and a short distance later it halted near a shrine. About twenty people had already assembled. They stood about a hundred meters away. I started feeling nervous. I adjusted my shirt and looked in the rear-view mirror to see if my hair was alright. I felt the paper-packet in my jeans pocket, which contained earrings for Shreya.

We moved towards them, Dr Iyer leading the way. I tried not to be self-conscious while walking. I began scanning the group from the left; she was not there. She was not in the middle. With a rocketing heart rate, I looked towards the right. How could that be possible? I looked about again, but she was nowhere. I recognised Shreya's parents but there was no sign of her.

And then I noticed the absence of the prospective groom himself. It could not be a prank. I was introduced by Professor Iyer as Rohit. 'Where is Rajit?' asked Dr Sidhu. 'Oh, he has gone to the market with his sister ...' That increased my agony and anger.

'Oh, I had a surprise for my son-in-law and you all,' said Dr Iyer, 'But since he is not here at the moment ... and the auspicious moment shouldn't pass ...'

He introduced Biobull majestically. Commotion and cries of congratulation followed. Everybody moved towards the bus as my frustration increased. Just then my mobile rang.

'Hullo, it is me, Rajit.'

'Thanks for calling.'

'Where are you?'

This was a fine question.

'Where else, the bus only just dropped me in Sri Lanka ...' I said nonchalantly.

'Shut up, Tej. What are you doing?'

'I am hatching a plot ...'

'What?'

'To disappear with your fiancé.'

'Look, let me explain this ...'

'I know the rules. You will count till fifty. Or is it hundred?'

'Do you realise we do not have time?'

'Oh! I thought we'd play Ring a Ring o' Roses next ...'

'Will you stop it?'

'Fine. Why else did you call me?'

'We are at the beach!'

'Oh, the beach! I thought you were headed for the mountains ...'

'Now shut up and pay attention! Your bus must have taken a left from ECR to reach that shrine. Come back onto the ECR and walk straight; another road will turn left after some distance. You'll see a board saying 'Private Road'. Don't worry about that, and walk right in. The road leads to the beach. Now come quick!'

'Oh, this is thrilling, but do we have enough guns in the case the enemy catches us?'

'You are one thankless fool, Tej. Did you want to meet Shreya first in front of a thousand people? Here I arrange a memorable rendezvous for you, and you go on and on with your nonsense.' It did not take long for me to recognise my bro-in-law's exemplary motives. He reminded me of Tanker.

I whispered to Prof. Pappi about the new development and darted off. I didn't know whether to run or to walk. And so I proceeded with a funny gait. As my nervousness increased, I took the turn with the 'Private Road' board. I saw Rajit standing far off, leaning against the wall; the road was quite long. I could see the beach but not the sea. I could only hear the waves. I walked quickly to Rajit and greeted him.

'Will you run to her?'

'Where are you going?'

'Do you want me to come?' he said bantering. 'You have ten minutes. You'll find me at that signboard. I'll keep an eye there.'

It was a scenic road with palatial houses on both sides. It opened on to the beach and I could only see the golden sand. As I walked, the sound of the waves became louder. I wondered what she would be wearing. I could see the waves rush to the shore now and my heart was filled with delight.

I was out in the open. I saw her walking by the sea, her hair blowing in the wind. She saw me and stopped. I started towards her. She remained where she was. She wore a white salwar-kameez, and a turquoise dupatta went around her neck and flew in the air with her hair. Her hair had grown a little longer. I reached her and looked into her brown eyes which were outlined by kajal. They were happy eyes. I took both her hands in mine and brought her closer, and she submitted herself to my arms. No one spoke, only the waves lent us their music. There was not a soul to be seen till eternity. I looked at the clear sky above and at the waves kissing our feet. It was pure bliss. I could feel her breathing against my chest. I felt something wet on my neck. I released her a little and saw her eyes. A lone tear had trickled down her cheek. I brought my lips to her cheek and kissed away the tear. The wind had gained momentum and the waves threatened to submerge our feet. I looked into her eyes, eyes that said so much. She closed them as I brought my lips close to hers and touched them. The wind, the waves, the sky, the day; had all ceased to exist.